"Sorry. I didn't expect anyone to be here."

Brodey's gaze traveled over her cashmere sweater, worn jeans and loafers, then came back up, lingering on her face, making her cheeks fire. *My goodness, the man has a way.* Had she known she'd be seeing anyone, particularly the intriguing detective, she'd have dressed more appropriately. But at 4:00 a.m., that thought hadn't crossed her mind.

"I couldn't sleep," she said. "The colors for the kitchen were driving me mad. Where's your sling?"

"You're here by yourself?"

"Of course."

"Anyone ever tell you it's dangerous for a woman to be driving around a city alone in the middle of the night?"

Prior to her panic a minute ago, she hadn't even questioned it. Maybe she should have. But that was the trusting part of her. The part that didn't include the male species and wanted to see pretty things instead of danger. She wasn't a complete lunatic and understood the world to be a dangerous place, but when it came to her creative process, certain things, like possible danger, couldn't get in her way. "I live ten minutes from here."

"A lot can happen in ten minutes."

THE DETECTIVE

USA TODAY Bestselling Author

ADRIENNE GIORDANO

Recycling programs
for this product may
not exist in your area.

ISBN-13: 978-0-373-74901-0

The Detective

Copyright © 2015 by Adrienne Giordano

Printed in U.S.A.

Adrienne Giordano, a *USA TODAY* bestselling author, writes romantic suspense and mystery. She is a Jersey girl at heart, but now lives in the Midwest with her workaholic husband, sports obsessed son and Buddy the wheaten terrorist (terrier). For more information on Adrienne's books, please visit adriennegiordano.com or download the Adrienne Giordano app. For information on Adrienne's street team, go to facebook.com/groups/dangerousdarlings.

Books by Adrienne Giordano

HARLEQUIN INTRIGUE

CAST OF CHARACTERS

Brodey Hayward—An overprotective (and slightly paranoid) Chicago homicide detective recruited by his private investigator sister to help solve the Jonathan Williams murder.

Alexis "Lexi" Vanderbilt—Chicago's up-and-coming interior designer hired to renovate the house of murder victim Jonathan Williams.

Jenna Hayward—Brodey's sister and a private investigator who works for Hennings & Solomon.

Brenda Williams—The murder victim's widow and mother to their three children.

Lawrence "Larry" McCall—A Chicago homicide detective assigned to the Jonathan Williams case.

Gerald Hennings—Senior partner from Hennings & Solomon and also Jenna's boss.

Pamela Hennings—The socialite wife of Gerald Hennings who volunteers Hennings & Solomon's investigators to help solve Jonathan Williams's murder.

Chapter One

Lexi Vanderbilt's mother taught her two very important lessons. One, always wear coordinating lipstick, and two, recognize an opportunity when it presented itself.

Standing in the ballroom of the newly renovated Gold Coast Country Club, Lexi planned on employing those lessons.

All around her workers prepared for the throng of club members who would descend in—she checked her watch—ninety-three minutes. As the interior designer about to unveil her latest masterpiece, she would spend those ninety-three minutes tending to everything from flowers to linens to centerpieces. A waiter toting a tray of sparkling champagne glasses cruised by. She took in the not-so-perfect cut of his tux and groaned. The staff's attire wasn't her jurisdiction. Still, small details never escaped her. At times, like now, it was maddening.

Oh, and just wait one second. "Excuse me,"

she said to a woman carrying a stack of table-cloths. "The sailboat ice sculpture belongs on the dessert table by the window. The Willis Tower goes by the champagne fountain."

The woman hefted the pile of linens, a not-so-subtle hint that the sculptures weren't her problem. "Does it matter?"

If it didn't, I wouldn't ask. Lexi sighed. "It matters. Unless you'd like to tell your boss, who specifically requested the placement of the sculptures, that it doesn't."

For added effect, Lexi grinned and the woman rolled her eyes. "I'll get the busboys to move it."

"Thank you."

One minicrisis averted. And maybe she could have let that one slide given that the club's manager had to be 110 years old and most likely wouldn't remember which sculpture went where, but why take a chance on something easily fixed?

Besides, tonight everything had to be perfect.

Functions attended by the richest of the rich were a breeding ground for opportunities. Opportunities Lexi craved for her fledgling design company. At twenty-nine, she'd already been profiled by the *Banner-Herald* and all the major broadcast stations in the city. She was quickly gaining ground on becoming Chicago's "it" designer, and that meant dethroning Jerome

Laddis, the current "it" designer. He may have had more experience, but Lexi had youth, energy and fresh ideas on her side. A few more insanely wealthy clients touting Lexi's work and *look out, Jerome.*

Then she'd hire an assistant, rehab her disaster of a garage into an office and get some sleep.

Lots of it.

Right now, as she glanced around, took in the exquisite silk drapes, the hundred-thousand-dollar chandelier and hand-scraped floor she'd had flown in from Brazil, no questions on the tiny details would haunt her. She'd make sure of it. Even if stress-induced hospitalization loomed in her near future.

The upshot? She'd lost five pounds in the past two weeks. Always a silver lining.

"Alexis?"

Lexi turned, her long gown swishing against the floor and snagging on her shoe. She smiled at Pamela Hennings while casually adjusting her dress. *Darned floor-length gowns.* "Mrs. Hennings, how nice to see you."

Mrs. Hennings air-kissed and stepped back. On her petite frame she wore a fitted gown in her signature sky blue that matched her eyes. The gown draped softly at the neckline, displaying minimal cleavage. As usual, a perfect choice.

"I love what you've done in here," Mrs. Hennings said. "Amazing job."

Being a club board member, she had no doubt shown up early to make sure the unveiling of the new room would be nothing short of remarkable. "Thank you. I enjoyed it. Just a few last-minute details and we'll be ready."

"Everything is lovely. Even the damned ice sculptures Raymond couldn't live without. Waste of money if you ask me, but some battles aren't worth fighting."

So true.

A loud bang from the corner of the room assaulted Lexi's ears. *Please let that be silverware.* She shifted her gaze left and spotted the waiter who'd passed her earlier scooping utensils onto a tray. *Thank you.*

Mrs. Hennings touched Lexi's arm. "By the bye, I think I have Gerald convinced his study needs an update. All that dark wood is depressing."

Now, *that* would be a thrill. If Lexi landed the job and nailed it, the top 10 percent of Chicago's executives would know it. And competition ran hot with this social set. Before long, they'd be lined up outside her office for a crack at outdoing Pamela and Gerald Hennings.

"I think," Lexi said, "for him we could leave

touches of the dark woods. Macassar ebony would be fabulous on the floor."

"Ooh, yes. Do you have time this week? Maybe you could come by and work up some sketches?"

"Of course." Lexi whipped her phone from her purse and scrolled to her calendar. "How about early next week? Tomorrow I'm starting a new project that might eat up the rest of my week."

"I'll make sure I'm available. What's this new project? Can you share?"

Rich folks. Always wanting the inside scoop. "Actually, it's quite fascinating. Remember the murdered broker?"

"The one from Cartright? How could I not? The entire neighborhood went into a panic."

The residents of Cartright, the North Side's closest thing to a gated community without the gates, employed private security to help patrol the six city blocks that made up their self-titled haven. That extra money spent on security kept the crime rate nearly nonexistent in those six city blocks.

Except for the offing of one crooked stock-broker.

"That's the one," Lexi said. "I've been hired to stage the house. The real-estate agent suggested it to the broker's widow and she hired me."

"I heard they couldn't sell. The market is destroying her. That poor woman. He left her with a mountain of trouble. He paid top dollar and if she lowers the price again, she won't make enough to clear his debts. Add to that any retribution owed to the clients he *borrowed* funds from without their knowledge."

As expected, Pamela Hennings was up to speed on the latest gossip. Gossip that Lexi would not share. Being told this information about a client was one thing. Sharing it? Not happening. "I'm looking forward to the project. It's an incredible house."

Being an interior designer didn't always give Lexi the chance to change someone's life. Her work allowed people to see the beauty in color and texture and shape and made their homes more than just a place to live, but she didn't often get the opportunity to alter an emotionally devastating situation. Now she had the chance. Getting this house sold would free the broker's widow from debt and give her children a comfortable life.

And Lexi wanted to see that happen.

Plus, if she got the thing sold in forty-five days, she'd make a whopping 20 percent bonus. The bonus alone would pay for an assistant and give her a life back.

Nap, here I come.

Mrs. Hennings made a tsk-tsk noise. "They never did find the murderer, did they?"

"No. Which I think is part of the problem. I may do a little of my feng shui magic in there. Clear all the negativity out. When I'm finished, that house will be beautiful and bright and homey."

"The debt, the children and now the police can't find the murderer. And it's been what, two years? No woman deserves to be left with that."

Again, Lexi remained quiet. *Don't get sucked in.* But, yes, it had been two years, and from what Lexi knew, the police were no closer to finding the man's killer. Such a tragedy. "The case has gone cold."

Sucked in. She smacked her lips together.

"You know," Mrs. Hennings said, "my husband's firm recently did some work with a pro bono cold case. I wonder if the investigator who worked on that wouldn't mind taking a look at this. I'd love to see the man's family given some relief. And, let's face it, it would certainly be good PR for the firm."

It certainly would.

Investigative help wouldn't hurt the real-estate agent's chances—or Lexi's—of getting the house sold in forty-five days. "Do you think they'd be interested?"

"Oh, I'm sure it can be arranged."

Gerald Hennings, aka the Dapper Defense Lawyer, pushed through the oversize ballroom doors, spotted the two women and unleashed a smile. Even in his sixties, he had charm to spare. Salt-and-pepper hair and the carved cheekbones of a man who'd once been devastatingly handsome—all combined with his intelligence—added up to someone who ruled a courtroom.

"Gerald," Mrs. Hennings said, "perfect timing. The board meeting will be upstairs. Believe it or not, we're the first ones here."

The Dapper DL eyed his wife with a hint of mischief, smiling in a rueful way that probably slayed jurors. "Shocking." Then he turned his charm loose on Lexi. "Alexis Vanderbilt, how are you?"

"I'm fine, Mr. Hennings. Thank you. And yourself?"

"I was quite well until fifteen seconds ago when my wife announced my timing was perfect. That means I'll either be writing you a healthy check or she's volunteered me for something. Either way, I'm sure it will be painful."

BRODEY HAYWARD BLEW out a breath as he watched his sister saunter into the Hennings & Solomon reception area. Finally she'd stopped wearing her blouses unbuttoned to her belly button. He never needed to see that much of Jenna's skin and said a silent thanks to whichever saint covered brothers in distress.

Jenna stopped in front of him and gave him a half hug so she didn't bump his sling and the wrecked arm inside of it.

"Nice shirt," he said.

She waved him off. "Don't start."

Hey, he couldn't help it if he had opinions. "Just commenting is all."

"How's the elbow?"

"It works."

"So, it's killing you."

He didn't bother answering. What good would it do? Six weeks ago he'd blown out his elbow changing a damned tire. The guys at the precinct tore that one up. *Hey, Hayward, helluva way to go out on disability. Hey, Hayward, you'd better make up a better story. Hey, Hayward, real detectives don't get hurt changing a tire.* Each day a slew of texts came in from his squad mates, and it didn't look as if the taunting would end soon because the surgery on his elbow left him with a raging infection that earned him a second surgery and another six weeks of leave. Leave that was slowly, deliberately, driving him insane. Torture was the only way to describe the abundance of nothingness that filled his days. As a homicide detective, he could tolerate a lot of things.

Boredom was not one of them.

Hell, he'd even taken to driving to his parents' house each day for cop talk with his retired detective father. A week into that, his mother had booted him and told him to get a life.

Thanks, Mom.

Jenna motioned him down the long corridor. "Thanks for coming in first thing. We're meeting in the conference room. You sure you're okay with this?"

"Yeah. I'm not getting paid. All I'm doing is giving you my opinion, right?"

"Right."

"Then I'm not violating any rules."

Jenna—a private investigator for Hennings & Solomon—had called him the night before asking if he'd assist on a cold case that somehow landed in her lap. Why not? He could kill time—no pun intended—and keep his mind sharp for his eventual return to the job. Plus, there'd be no emotional involvement with this case. Technically, it wasn't his, so he could walk away without running himself through a meat grinder over it.

"Good. I've looked over all the files, but I'm missing something."

Brodey followed Jenna while eyeing the art lining the walls. Some would call it modern. He'd call it weird with all those slashes of color, but whatever. Art meant a real picture of something. A woman in a park, a kid flying a kite, something he could look at and recognize. This hoity-toity stuff, he didn't get.

They reached the conference room, where a huge whiteboard smothered with notes and charts covered one wall. His sister had been busy. She'd also done a fine job of organizing her evidence.

She gestured to the wall. "I have it all laid out for you. Just the way Dad taught us."

He wandered to the board and glanced at Jenna's notes. Victim's name, Jonathan Williams. Scene of the crime, brownstone on the cushy North Side. Cause of death, gunshot to the head.

"Crime-scene photos?"

"No. I was hoping you or Dad could help with that."

Not if he wanted to stay under the radar he couldn't. "I'll talk to Dad. Tell me again how you got this case."

"It's kind of convoluted."

"It always is, Jenna."

"Remember how I worked on Brent's mom's murder case a few months back?"

How could a guy forget Brent, the giant deputy US marshal who had stolen his sister's heart *and* managed to convince her she didn't need to walk around half-naked for people to notice her?

Brent had enough baggage to fill a 747 jet and Jenna had still fallen in love with him. If nothing else, it showed a boy could overcome a rotten childhood and grow into an honorable man.

"So this has to do with Brent?"

"No. Mrs. Hennings. She was the one who convinced my boss to take on Brent's case. She's at it again with this one."

Did someone say *convoluted*? *"Oooookay."*

"Mrs. Hennings attended a social function and ran into a decorator she knows."

Brodey gawked. A *decorator*? This should be good.

Jenna held her hand up before he could crack wise. "The decorator was hired by a real-estate agency to stage the house of the murder victim. The house has been on the market for two years and they're about to drop the price. Before they did that, the victim's estranged wife—they were separated, but not yet divorced—wanted to try redecorating it. I suppose when a house is worth close to two million hiring a decorator isn't an issue."

Brodey let out a low whistle. "I'll say. Why am I here?"

"The decorator told Mrs. Hennings about the house, and here we are."

"What do you get out of it?"

"My boss's undying gratitude for keeping him out of trouble with his wife."

Brodey laughed. One thing about Jenna, she knew how to stay on a man's good side. He pointed to the board. "Whatcha got?"

"You may remember this case. He was a stockbroker living the good life until the market crashed. For years he'd basically been running a Ponzi scheme with his clients' money. His marriage fell apart and he was drowning in debt. The FBI eventually caught up to him and he was under investigation."

"He was murdered before the Feds charged him, right? Is that the guy?"

"Yes. On the day his body was found, he didn't show up for a meeting with his biggest client. That was unusual so his firm called his wife. Apparently he hadn't updated his emergency contact at the office so her cell phone was the only number they had."

"Ah, damn. Don't tell me the ex found him."

Jenna nodded. "In the laundry room."

Poor woman. Brodey still hadn't gotten used to viewing murder victims' bodies, inhaling that nasty metallic odor of blood and trying to remain unaffected. Forget about a loved one. That? No way.

Refusing to give in to his thoughts, Brodey stood, arms folded, studying the board. "I think

I remember this. Looked like a robbery gone bad, right?"

"Yes. In the two years since the murder, the widow has spent most of the insurance money settling their debts, but she's not in the clear yet. It's a mess. With the divorce pending, the finances hadn't been worked out. The house was paid off, but she can't unload it and needs the cash."

"Enter our illustrious decorator."

Jenna gave him a snarky grin. "You're so smart."

Whatever, wisenheimer. "The house is empty?"

"Yes. Why?"

He waved at the board. "No photos. I don't know what you want me to do without seeing the crime scene."

His sister should have known he'd need photos or some kind of visual. Or maybe that was just the way *his* mind worked. Needing to see how the crime occurred, run the scenarios, figure the timing and options. All of it helped him work a case.

"I wasn't sure how involved you wanted to be."

Outside of being bored out of his skull, he *didn't* want to be involved. He'd made detective only a year ago and wasn't about to aggravate his boss by poking around in another guy's case.

This case wasn't even his jurisdiction. This belonged to the North Side guys, while he worked Area Central.

"Yeah, but I can't help you if I don't know what I'm dealing with. Take me to the house. I'll walk through it and then study what you have here. Then I'll tell you what I think, and I'm out."

Tops, he was looking at two days of research. Two days of not being bored. Two days of getting closer to the end of his disability leave.

All he had to do was pony up an opinion and send his little sister on her way.

Piece of cake.

Chapter Two

Lexi stood in the expansive living room of the Williamses' brownstone studying carpet that made her think of dirty snow. Such an abomination. What were they thinking putting that disgusting carpet in this house? Given the budget constraints, she'd have to keep it simple, but she could, without a doubt, restore the house to its classic elegance. Flooring she'd splurge on because the situation begged for hardwood. Everywhere else she'd do subtle but warm paint colors and effective accents with doorknobs, handrails and fixtures.

"Every inch of this carpet has to come up," she said to Nate, the contractor she'd chosen for this job. "I'm betting there's hardwood underneath."

And, if it could be salvaged, it would help her budget.

Nate made notes on his clipboard as they wandered through the house. She liked Nate.

They'd worked together on several projects, and although he was closing in on fifty, he had the mind of a thirty-year-old. When he did a renovation, he saw youth and exuberance, and his attention to detail and superior craftsmanship made him her go-to guy on important projects.

She moved through the kitchen—again with the dirty snow? This time it was on the walls. She had nothing against light beige. Neutrals with the right texture and undertones—wisps of green, yellow or orange—gave a room dimension. *Depth.* This beige?

Awful.

"We'll be repainting in here."

"Just tell me what colors."

"Let's do that soft gray we did in the Wileys' kitchen. We'll add color splashes to brighten it up. It'll be fabulous with the natural light."

"Got it."

The laundry room off the kitchen came next, and she hesitated at the doorway. Did Nate know a man had been murdered in here? The real-estate agent had assured Lexi the scene had been sanitized, but what made her nervous, made that little twitch in her cheek fire, was what had seeped *beneath* the tile. When they tore up that floor, would they find dried blood?

Lexi reached in and groped along the wall for the light switch. *Where are you? Got it.* The room, roughly ten by ten, lit up, its glossy white walls glowing. A built-in closet with shelves and coat hooks and storage bins lined one wall. The opposite wall housed the washer and dryer.

How odd that the only room not needing updating was the one room she'd been directed to completely redesign.

Then again, a dead body tended to destroy positive energy. She glanced at the floor, imagined Jonathan Williams sprawled across the slate-look porcelain and closed her eyes, hoping to clear that nasty image. A dead body definitely killed creativity. *Ditch the body.* She opened her eyes again. "I'd like to know what's under the tile. It's a shame they want this redone. With all the traffic that comes through here, porcelain is perfect." She waggled her fingers. "Give me your hammer. Please."

The tile had to come up anyway and, well, she didn't want to stress about what had seeped under there. She'd find out now. Face it head-on, as she did any other issue.

Nate pulled the hammer from his tool belt and handed it over. She squatted, ready to administer that first whack, when the front door chime sounded. Someone coming in.

"You expecting someone?" Nate asked.

"No. Hello?" she hollered.

No response. A few seconds later a man appeared—and what a man he was with all that lush dark hair. He wore a sling on his right arm, flat-front khakis and a white button-down shirt under a leather jacket. The arm in the sling was tucked under the jacket, his sleeve hanging loose. His lace-up oxfords were just the right touch. Not too formal, not too casual. His dark emerald eyes zoomed in on the hammer and his jaw—really nice, strong jaw—locked. Modern-day Indiana Jones here.

He stepped forward. "What the hell do you think you're doing?"

"Excuse me?"

Grabbing the hammer with his free hand, he gave it back to Nate. "You can't do that."

"I most certainly can. Who're you?"

"Who're *you*? Wait. Don't tell me. You're the *decorator*."

Oh, and the way he said it. All sarcastic and snippy as if she was some dope. Some airhead incapable of forming a sentence. She breathed in, counted to three and stood tall. "I'm the *interior designer*. Alexis Vanderbilt. Hired by the owner of this home to do my magic. That includes tearing up this tile. Something I'd rather not do, but when a client makes a request, I generally respond."

"Brodey?" A woman called from the front of the house.

Brodey. Had Brenda Williams mentioned a Brodey? Lexi ticked names off in her mind. No Brodey.

"Back here," Brodey Whoever said. "I just met the decorator."

"Well, technically, we haven't *met*. All you've done is come in here and make unreasonable demands."

That made Brodey Whoever smile, and it wasn't just one of those run-of-the-mill, see-it-every-day smiles. *This* smile developed slowly, like a growing—and sometimes devastating—wave. *Hello, smile.*

"You're right," he said. "My apologies. I'm Brodey Hayward. I'd shake your hand, but…"

He gestured to his sling just as a stunning brunette stepped behind him. When the brunette spotted Nate and Lexi, her head jerked back. "Oh, hello."

Now might be as good a time as any for Lexi to take up meditation. "Excuse me, but who are you people?"

The brunette angled around Brodey and stuck her hand out. "I'm Jenna Hayward from Hennings & Solomon. I'm a private investigator assisting on Mr. Williams's case. I believe you're aware we'd be helping. This is my brother Brodey. He's a—"

"I'm helping," Brodey interrupted, clearly not wanting his sister to explain.

How very interesting. Mental note: do an internet search on Brodey Hayward.

The investigators. *Got it.* Lexi shook Jenna's hand. "Right. I'm sorry. Mrs. Williams hadn't mentioned you were coming by today. We should be done in the next hour or so. Feel free to ignore us. Now, if you'll step back, I need to see what's under this tile." She flopped her hand out to Nate. "Hammer, please?"

"I don't think so," Brodey said.

"Pardon?"

"An unsolved murder occurred in this room. Could be potential evidence under there." He jerked his thumb to the kitchen. "How about working around this area until I can look at it?"

Again, Lexi breathed deep. Channeled her inner calm. "Mr. Hayward—"

"Brodey is fine."

"Brodey. Great. Thank you. Now, I'm sure the Chicago Police Department has been through here." She waggled her hands. "They have all their crime-scene people and whatnot. After all, this house has been empty for two years."

Two years without an offer because potential buyers were spooked about the murder in a supposed high-security community.

Imitating her gesture, Brodey waggled his

hand. "If it's been empty all that time, another hour won't hurt." He stepped aside. "If you'll excuse us, we have work to do."

The inner warrior in Lexi didn't just yell, she roared. Frustration railed, turning her vision a starker white than the glossy walls. She didn't care what kind of an investigator Brodey Hayward was. Treating them like rodents would not do. *Relax. This is not a problem until you make it one.* Lexi swung to Nate. "Would you give us a minute, please?"

He nodded. "Sure thing."

Jenna, the beautiful brunette, stepped aside, smiling at Nate as he gave her more—much more—than a brief once-over. She smiled, but averted her eyes, letting Nate know in expert fashion he should forget about her and keep on moving. Nice move on her part. But right now, Lexi needed to strike a deal. Figure out how long they needed to be here and when she could start tearing the place apart. Compromise. That was what she'd do.

"Brodey, I'm trying to get this house redesigned and sold in forty-five days. Do you have any idea what an undertaking that is?"

He smiled at her, a slow, cocky grin that would surely lead to a sarcastic remark. "I'm sure you're being well compensated."

Bingo. Everyone liked to rip on the *decorator*.

How she hated that word. As if her bachelor's in interior design coupled with her master's in business didn't qualify her for the Intelligent Club. "Okay, well, just so you know, it's a *huge* undertaking. But I'll get it done. I'm a woman with the promised land in sight and I *want* the promised land. Tell me how long you need to be in here and I'll see if I can make that happen."

"So, all you care about is selling this house? Doesn't matter that a guy bled out in here?"

Of course it mattered. That was the point. "That's not what I meant, and you know it. This place has been a financial drain on Mrs. Williams. And, simply put, I like her and she deserves a break. If we get the house sold, she can put her children's lives back together. If that's even possible."

Behind Brodey, his sister was all big blue eyes taking in not just every word, but every vowel, and Lexi didn't like an audience. She sighed, grasped the sleeve of Brodey's jacket and drew him into the kitchen away from Jenna.

Once in the far corner, Lexi let go of him and folded her arms. "We've definitely gotten off to a bad start here. I want to help you. I do. And it's not about my compensation."

Not entirely.

Brodey, quite handsome in his khaki pants and button-down shirt, studied her. Typically, she didn't go for noncorporate guys. And it had nothing to do with her being a snob. Not one bit. Her world revolved around the ultra-wealthy, and with that came an acceptance of spending ridiculous amounts of cash on items most people couldn't afford to spend ridiculous amounts of cash on. Regular Joes tended to scoff at twenty-thousand-dollar sofas. For up-and-coming executives, it was the norm.

And they didn't think her frivolous for it.

But something about Brodey Hayward's dark green eyes made her think of fresh air, lazy days and picnics by the lake. Something she hadn't allowed herself in a long—very long—time. Her business had taken priority in her life. Yes, she dated, had even thought she'd fallen in love once. At least until she found her up-and-coming executive across his desk exploring his intern's anatomy. Such a cliché.

Brodey cocked his head and grinned. "You were saying?"

She held up one finger. "Right. Yes. I was *saying* that each day this house sits on the market, Mrs. Williams is one step closer to financial ruin. I can help change that, but it won't happen overnight. I need to tear up floors and repaint. I need to dismantle part of the house."

"And destroy possible evidence."

She gritted her teeth. "Which is not my intention. Are you always this way?"

"What way?"

"Contrary."

He shrugged. "I'm a cop."

Lexi dipped her head forward. "You're a cop? I thought you were a private investigator?"

"No. Jenna is the PI. I'm a homicide detective. Chicago PD."

"Oh."

"But, I'm not on this case in an official capacity. I'm giving my sister an opinion. That's all. I'm here to look at the scene and then I'm gone."

"You could have said that. I mean, we went through this whole thing and you're here for a quick visit?"

"There might still be evidence somewhere. Particularly in that laundry room."

She'd say one thing about Brodey Hayward—the man had a spine. And the way he stood there, shoulders back, so confident and, well, *commanding*, even in a sling, she didn't think for one second he'd let her take a hammer to that tile.

This might take a while. Lexi turned back and peered at the laundry room doorway, where Jenna put her thumbs to work on her phone. "Well, maybe I could work around that room. For now. How much time do you need?"

"I'm not sure."

"Now you're just being annoying."

Brodey laughed. "Maybe. But it's partially true. Give me an hour and we'll see what's what. Is that a deal?"

"One hour?"

"Yes."

"Deal."

Chapter Three

An hour turned into two and Brodey wasn't done. He squatted in the laundry room, ran his free hand over a chipped edge of grout. Without the actual case file outlining the details of the crime scene, he couldn't form any solid opinions.

He was flying blind. In the dark. Although, if he was flying blind, it would already be dark.

And, hell no, he would not get sucked into this. He'd give an opinion. That was it. Unfortunately, giving an opinion required a basic understanding of the case.

"I need the case file," he said to Jenna.

His sister stood in the doorway, leaning against the door frame. "I don't have that."

"I still need it."

Maybe he could cash in on a couple of favors. Or his father could. Being a retired detective, the old man had more contacts in the department. And it would keep Brodey off the radar.

Alexis strode into the kitchen, her sky-high heels clicking on the tile. "How's it going?"

Even on those heels, he looked down at her. Judging by his six-foot-one size, he'd put her at around five-four. Five-five if he wanted to be generous.

Alexis Vanderbilt.

Vanderbilt.

Her name stank of money. Seriously, how many women walked around in five-inch heels, a pair of tight-fitting black pants that made a man's mind go wild and a blazer over—get this—a leather halter-top-looking thing. Who did that?

Nobody Brodey knew. That was for sure.

But he kinda liked it. From a purely male point of view.

"It's not going," he said.

"Excuse me?"

"I need to talk to your client."

Jenna stepped farther into the room to make way for Alexis. "I could have Mr. Hennings contact her."

Alexis dragged her phone from her jacket pocket. "I'll call her."

Maybe the sexy decorator wasn't so bad after all. Brodey grinned. "Thank you."

She gave him a sarcastic, bunchy-cheeks grin. "It has nothing to do with your enormous

charm. It'll be faster if I call her. By the time
Jenna tracks down her boss and he calls my
client, you could be on your way over there. I'm
all for efficiency."

That made two of them. And when efficiency looked like Alexis Vanderbilt, prefera-
bly a naked Alexis Vanderbilt because yeah, he
was wondering what that looked like, he'd welcome it any day, any time without a doubt. Pro-
fessionalism aside, he was still a guy who liked
action. Plenty of it.

"Brenda?" Alexis said into her phone. "Hi.
It's Lexi Vanderbilt...yes...I'm fine."

Lexi. He liked that. It fit with her sassy attitude. She bobbed her head while going through
the pleasantries with her client and Brodey sur-
mised that, like him, she had issues being idle.
For any length of time.

"Yes," she said. "I'm at the house now. There
are two investigators here from Hennings &
Solomon."

Technically, Brodey wasn't from Hennings
& Solomon, but he'd let that go. Not worth the
hassle.

"They got here a couple of hours ago," Lexi
continued, "and they have questions for you.
Would you be able to speak with them?"

Three seconds passed. Then she handed
Brodey the phone. He immediately looked at

his sister, waggling the phone at her to make sure she didn't want to take the lead. She shook her head.

Excellent answer. Not that he would have minded her taking the call, but when the phone hit his hand he got that familiar push of adrenaline, that spark that came with a fresh case and the possibility of leads. At the age of thirty-two, he hadn't been a detective long enough to turn jaded. The older guys on the squad liked to call him Greenhorn. Being the youngest—and newest—detective to join his squad, he still viewed every case as an opportunity to make a difference while the old guys hoped to retire with their sanity. Twenty years of working homicides on the streets of Chicago would emotionally annihilate even the toughest of the tough. Brodey hoped to retire long before annihilation occurred and already had a start on a healthy nest egg.

He held the phone to his ear. "Mrs. Williams, this is Brodey Hayward. Thank you for taking my call."

There was a short pause and Brodey checked the screen to make sure the call hadn't dropped. Nope. Still there. "Hello?"

"Yes," she said. "I'm here. I needed to step into the other room. My youngest is playing and I didn't want her to hear."

The youngest, according to Jenna, had been three when her father died. So, she'd be five now and Brodey tried to imagine that, tried to imagine growing up without his own father, without the memories of ball games and amusement parks and beach visits. All of it a dead loss. Poor kids. A squeeze in his chest ambushed him and he held his breath a second, waited for the pressure to ease before exhaling and clearing his throat.

Stay focused. Forget the kids. That was what he needed to do. "No problem. Are you able to answer some questions for me? I could drop by."

Because really, what he wanted to see was her. Study her body language and responses. Call him cynical, even as a rookie detective, but the spouse—particularly an estranged one—always got a solid look.

"Now?"

"Yes, ma'am. If it's convenient."

"I need to pick up my son from school and then take him to basketball practice at four-thirty. Lexi is coming by at four with samples. I can't imagine that will take long. I could meet with you then, also. Would that work?"

He wasn't sure how Lexi would feel about that, but in his mind, murder trumped decorating, so he'd make an executive decision. "I'll make it work, ma'am. Thank you."

Brodey disconnected and handed Lexi the phone. "We're riding shotgun on your four o'clock."

"Say again?"

"She said you were meeting with her at four and we could meet with her then, too. She's busy running kids around. We need to maximize our time."

"She only gave me thirty minutes."

"She's now splitting that thirty minutes between us. You'll need to shorten your list."

SHORTEN HER LIST? Brodey Hayward had a serious superiority complex if he thought she'd let him dictate how to do her job. First he horned in on her meeting and now he was trying to take over?

"Uh, Brodey?" Jenna said from her spot against the wall. "I can't meet with her at four. I have another meeting."

Thank you. At least now Lexi would still get her measly thirty minutes for what could evolve into a two-hour discussion.

Brodey turned to his sister, his posture stiff and unyielding. He held his uninjured arm out. "What do you want to do, then?"

"Hey," Jenna shot, "don't get snippy with me. You're the one who booked a meeting without checking my schedule. If you want to meet with her on your own, go to it. All I'm saying is I can't be there."

"I'm not getting snippy."

"Yes, you are."

And now the two of them were going to argue. Terrific. Lexi held her hand up. "Can you two fight about this later?"

"We're not fighting," Brodey said.

Patience. Lexi squeezed her eyes shut, begging her beloved and departed grandmother to channel some of her legendary patience. Just a bit. Lexi had inherited her gram's artistic ability, as evidenced by the stack of patchwork quilts she kept in her closet, but she'd be selfish now and ask for patience, too. Just a little. She breathed in and opened her eyes.

"For the record," Brodey said, "if we were fighting, there'd be yelling."

Jenna nodded. "And I might throw something."

"That's true. She gave me a black eye with a hockey puck once. And somehow, I got in trouble. Figure that one out." He stepped over to her, lifted his arm, the one in the sling, and winced. "Ow. Forgot about the bum arm."

"Ha!" Jenna said. "That's what you get for thinking you'd give me a noogie."

"I wasn't."

"Liar. I know you. And now that you're injured, you're a lame duck. Lame, I tell you."

He and Jenna both laughed. And just that fast—*boom*—the tension flew from the room.

Being the only child of an artist and a musician, both of whom enjoyed their alone time, Lexi hadn't experienced sibling rivalry. She wasn't sure she wanted to, but this? This was different. This was about love and family and history. As much as she wanted to be irritated with these two, watching them snark at each other and then laugh about it tickled something down deep.

But she wouldn't show them that. Instead, she rolled her eyes. "Okay, you're not fighting. Glad we cleared that up. What are we doing about this meeting at four?"

"I'll do it alone." Brodey turned back to Jenna. "You sure you're okay with that? It's your case."

"It's fine. Just make sure she knows you're only helping. I don't want her upset when you disappear."

"I will." He faced Lexi and pulled a pocket notepad from his jacket. "I guess it's you and me. Where am I meeting you?"

Chapter Four

Brenda Williams's two-story house butted up against the neighboring homes and looked like any other on the block. Weathered brick, a few steps leading to the small porch that barely spanned the front door, a single large window facing the street on the first floor, all of it as ordinary and indistinguishable as every other structure on the block.

Without a doubt, a long way from the pristine five-thousand-square-foot, multimillion-dollar greystone she'd shared with her husband. That house screamed vintage details on the outside but modern upgrades on the inside. To say the least, Brenda Williams had downsized. Apparently not by choice.

A wicked January wind whipped under Brodey's open jacket to the blasted sling. Leave it to him to screw up his arm in the dead of winter. Despite the doc's cautions, Brodey had been ditching the sling for an hour or two each day to give himself some freedom. That hour happened earlier when his shoulder cramped up. Now he was stuck in the sling for the remainder of the day. Unless he wanted his doctor to rail on him. *What he doesn't know won't hurt him.*

He stepped to the side of the concrete walkway leading to the porch and waved Lexi forward. "Do the honors."

She climbed the stairs, her long coat covering her amazing rear, and on any day he'd call that one of the great tragedies of his lifetime. And that was saying something for a Chicago PD homicide detective.

Twisted perhaps, but hey, the little things kept a guy like him sane.

Lexi rapped on the door, then turned back. "Did you say something?"

Could be. While working a case he talked to himself. A lot. "Probably."

She wrinkled her nose. "I'm sorry?"

"I talk to myself. I work crime scenes by talking my way through them, trying to figure out what happened. Half the time I don't know I'm doing it." *Like now.* "What did I say?"

Because given his lack of focus on anything but her delectable rear, he could easily be accused of lascivious thoughts. Thoughts he'd never deny when it came to a woman who looked like Lexi Vanderbilt.

"You were mumbling something about tragedies."

Phew. Easy one. "Ah. I was thinking about this house versus the one we left. The whole situation is tragic."

"That it is."

The front door eased open and a petite brunette wearing jeans, boots and a long gray sweater greeted them. She wore her shoulder-length hair tucked behind her ears, and minimal eye makeup accented her brown eyes. Beautiful eyes. Big and round and probably at one time alluring to any man. All he saw now was sadness.

"Hi, Lexi."

"Hi, Brenda. We're a little early. I hope that's all right."

"It's fine. But I just got home, so I'll need a minute. Come in."

Brodey followed Lexi into the foyer, where a blast of warm air thawed him. Directly in front of them a staircase with an oak rail and cool twisted spindles led to the second floor. To his left, through a set of glossy white French doors, was the living room.

Children's voices carried from the end of the

hallway. Kitchen probably. Most of these row houses were built with the same basic layout. Living room, small dining room, kitchen on the first floor. Three bedrooms upstairs. He'd lay money on it.

Lexi spun back to him. "Brodey Hayward, this is Brenda Williams."

"Hello, ma'am. I'd shake your hand, but…" He pointed to his bad arm.

"That must be horrible in this cold. Aren't you freezing?"

"It's not bad."

No sense in complaining about it. In the grand scheme, he could count his problems in three seconds or less, and that alone was enough to be thankful for.

Brenda led them down the long hallway to the back of the house where the kitchen—*called it*—conjoined with a small sitting area. Didn't call *that* one, but he was close enough. That particular room must have been a modification to the original floor plan. That was what he'd go with.

An older boy of about eleven sat with two girls at the round kitchen table. Table for four. The boy met Brodey's eyes, and nothing in his gaze conveyed anything he should see in a pre-teen boy's expression. No mischief, no relaxed demeanor, no lightness. All he saw there was suspicion. A shame, that.

The girl with long blond hair kept her gaze focused on her notebook. Not even a glance at him. The other girl, the one with her brown hair in a ponytail, gave him a cursory once-over and managed a whisper of a smile. Cripes, these kids were locked up tight. Of the three, he guessed the order of ages would be the boy, blonde girl and then ponytail rounding out the pack.

"Sam," Mrs. Williams said, "please take the kids upstairs to play for a few minutes while I speak with Miss Lexi and Mr. Brodey. We need to leave in half an hour, so make sure you have everything."

The boy glanced up, his big eyes drooping and, well...miserable. Suppressed. "Okay," he said. "C'mon, guys. Let's go."

The kids left, shuffling out of the room like obedient soldiers, and to Brodey, none of it seemed right. When he was a kid, all they did was yell and run around and get hollered at. They were kids. Kids did stuff like that. This? He didn't know what this was. Check that. He did know.

This was decimation.

Mrs. Williams watched them go, her gaze glued to them. "It's a sad day when the eleven-year-old becomes the man of the house."

"That it is."

She slid into the chair her son had vacated. "Please, have a seat. I thought we'd work in here so we could spread Lexi's samples out."

Would it be rude if he groaned? Probably. But he was a damned homicide detective. What did he know about decorating? He dragged a chair out for Lexi. "You first?"

With any luck, she'd disagree, which was what he really wanted, but since he'd already crashed her meeting he might as well at least try to be accommodating. Even if he hoped it went the other way.

She shook her head. "No. You go first."

The decorator is growing on me. He gave her chair a gentle push and walked to the other side of the table next to Mrs. Williams.

"What can I help you with, Mr. Hayward?"

From across the table, Lexi handed him the legal pad he'd asked her to stow in her briefcase. Using his usual pocket notepad was impossible with one arm in the sling. Another reason he needed to deep-six the thing. He angled the pad on his lap so he could write on it without disrupting the elbow too much. "It's Brodey. I have questions. Basic timeline stuff. I'm sure it's in the case file, but Hennings & Solomon doesn't have access to those files."

"Of course. Whatever you need."

"You separated from your husband a few months before his death. Is that right?"

"Yes. Two months. Things in the marriage had been off. For a while. We tried therapy, but he was so distracted with work, it was a wasted effort. Toward the end, I couldn't stand his moodiness and the children were miserable. I knew we had to get out." She waved her hands around the room. "We found this place and moved in."

Brodey jotted notes, taking a few seconds to get his thoughts in order. Distracted husband. Any number of things could cause that. Money, job in jeopardy, gambling, drugs, an affair. "Were his work distractions typical?"

"Yes and no. He'd always been obsessed with his job, but that last year was worse. When I asked about it, he continually put me off. I knew something was wrong. I just didn't know what. After he died, I found out he was stealing from his clients, basically using their money to fuel our lifestyle."

And, hello, fraud investigation. "How?"

"Every time he signed a new client, he'd take money from their account. He'd keep part of it and then pay dividends to existing clients with the rest." She squeezed her eyes closed and shook her head. "My husband ran a Ponzi scheme." She opened her eyes, stared right into Brodey's. "We lived on stolen money."

Beside him, Lexi shifted, played with her fingers, staring down at them as if fascinated. She needed a poker face. But, in her defense, the average citizen should be uncomfortable with this conversation. Not Brodey. To him, this was nothing. "Do you know if he'd received any threats prior to his death?"

"I don't know. The police asked me, but I was such an idiot—completely in the dark. I know we had a plan. At least I did. I wanted that happily-ever-after. Only, my husband turned out to be a liar and a thief. I'm not the one who committed a crime, but I'm left with the fallout and the paralyzing debt. I guess you could say my plan blew up."

Sure did.

She shrugged. "I'm trying to make it right. As much as I can anyway. My kids don't deserve this, and I'm not sure how much to tell them. Sam is old enough to have suspicions, but he's never asked specific questions and I don't have it in me to tell him. Does that make me a strong parent or a weak one?"

Brodey wasn't sure she really wanted an answer and it probably wasn't his place to give one, but being naive didn't make her a criminal.

Unless, of course, she murdered her husband.

"I'd say it makes you human," he said. "You'll figure out what to tell them when the time is right."

She met his gaze and her eyebrows lifted a millimeter. Classic body language for surprise. Excellent. If he'd scored points, great, but in this situation, he was damned certain his answer was the right one for different reasons. Reasons that involved three kids who'd lost their father.

Williams was a schmuck, but he was their schmuck.

Brenda glanced at the oversize clock on the wall. "I'm sorry. We'll need to leave in a few minutes and I know Lexi had some samples for me."

"Of course," Brodey said. "Is it all right if I follow up with you in a day or so?"

"Certainly. And thank you. If we can, I'd like to know what happened to him. He wasn't a great husband, but I loved him. Whatever his sins, I loved him."

AT SIX-OH-FIVE Brodey hustled through his parents' front door and got the shock of his life.

Jenna and Brent, his sister's massive US marshal of a boyfriend, had beat him there. What the hell? On any normal day, he arrived early and they were late. Tonight, he needed them to be later than he was because one thing was for sure. If dinner was ready and you weren't there, they didn't wait.

No. Sir.

"Well, hell. The one time I'm late and you two can't throw me a bone and be even later than I am?"

Brent scooped a mountain of mashed potatoes onto his plate, then passed the bowl to Brodey's youngest brother, Evan. "My fault," he said. "Problem with my witness got squared away faster than I thought."

"Anything good?" Dad asked.

"Eh, death threat. Not on my shift, though. Shift before mine. I got him to a new location and headed back before the Eisenhower went schizo."

Brodey slid into his normal chair next to his mother just as the meat loaf hit his spot. But damn, he loved his mother's meat loaf.

"I swear," Mom said, "we cannot get through a meal in this house without some form of law-enforcement talk."

"Sorry, ma'am," Brent said.

"It's certainly not *your* fault."

Across from him, Jenna snatched a roll from the basket of bread and handed it over. "How'd you do today, Brodey? With the widow?"

Pretzel rolls. Mom had gone all the way tonight. He took two rolls and sent the basket to his father. "I need the case file. She says she didn't know anything until after he bit it. I think I believe her. Not sure. Dad, can you get me any notes on this thing?"

Before his father could answer, Jenna held her hand up. "What happened to you getting in and out quick?"

"Still goes. I'll look at the file, tell you what I think, then I'm gone. I'm still holding to my two days of research."

"She got to you."

"Stop it."

"Or maybe it was the kids."

He breathed in, sent his sister a glare. "Stop. It."

She elbowed Brent. "Told you this would happen. He's cooked. He must have seen those kids and his heart melted. I know my brother."

Dad snorted. "That you do, my angel."

Whatever. "Maybe I'm curious. I'm a detective doing my due diligence. The widow was cleared, but she's definitely angry."

Dad swallowed a mouthful of food and waved his fork. "You like the widow for this?"

"I don't see her taking this guy out, but she should get another look. See what's what."

Dad did his quasi head tilt/nod. "After dinner I'll make a couple of calls. See who can get a copy of a report or two. You never know."

Exactly what he'd walked in here needing. His father always came through. Always. "Thanks, Dad." He looked across to his sister, who eyed him like a tiger on prey. "I'm not denying I saw those kids and all I could think was they got screwed out of ball games and fishing trips with their father." He poked himself in the chest. "I got that. They didn't. Doesn't seem fair."

"It's not fair," Jenna said. "That's why I knew you couldn't walk away from this. Family is too important to you."

What the hell did that mean? "You played me?"

She grinned. "Only a little."

His little sister, the conniver. And a damned good investigator. "At least you admit it. After today, we're in this together. You, me and decorator Lexi."

Chapter Five

Dawn broke just as Lexi finished sketching the Williamses' kitchen. She stood at the center island, random sheets of discarded sketches strewn around her. Half the night she'd stewed over the color of the kitchen walls until finally, unable to visualize the finished product—something that rarely happened anymore—she'd dragged herself out of bed, grabbed her sketching tools and drove to the house.

Here she'd be able to create a sketch and add the color variations until she found the perfect combination. When all else failed, her artistic ability, her skill in re-creating a room by hand drawing it, always came through. Unfortunately for her, this time it happened at 4:00 a.m. when she'd had next to no sleep. But if sleep wouldn't come, she'd do what she always did and work.

And with the lost time due to the Hennings & Solomon people—Brodey Hayward specifically—she needed to get moving on this project or risk blowing that forty-five-day deadline.

She glanced at the window above the sink, where morning sun peeped through the wooden blinds. Streaks of burnt orange splashed across the countertop in neat little rows, their perfection beautiful and uniform. Using pencils and charcoal, she shaded the area around the window, then added a touch of tangerine. Instantly the drawing came to life. Excitement bloomed in the pit of her stomach and launched upward as her fingers flew across the sketch, then switching colors, shading, switching colors again and filling in accents. All of it combining to create a visual of a room that would be homey, bright and warm.

Finally, after an hour of discarding sketches, she'd hit on it and now, with the sun rising, she moved faster, trying to capture every nuance, every shadow, every angle, before the light changed.

The long, shrill tone of the alarm sounded— door opening—and Lexi shot upright, pencil still in hand. Someone was here. She'd locked the door, hadn't she? Sometimes she forgot that little task, but even she wouldn't be foolish enough to walk into a strange house at four in the morning and not lock the door.

The buhm-buhm of her heart kicked up, a

slow-moving panic spreading through her body. Had she locked that damned door?

A second later Brodey stepped into the doorway, his head snapping back at the sight of her. He wore black track pants and a heavy sweatshirt. No jacket in this cold? The man was insane. His sling was gone and he held a manila envelope in his left hand.

Lexi blew out a hard breath and tossed her pencil on the counter. "Goodness' sake, Brodey. You scared me."

"Sorry. I didn't expect anyone to be here."

His gaze traveled over her cashmere sweater, worn jeans and loafers, then came back up, lingering on her face, making her cheeks fire. My goodness, the man had a way. Had she known she'd be seeing anyone, particularly the intriguing detective, she'd have dressed more appropriately. But at 4:00 a.m. that thought hadn't crossed her mind.

"I couldn't sleep," she said. "The colors for the kitchen were driving me mad. Where's your sling?"

"You're here by *yourself*?"

"Of course."

"Anyone ever tell you it's dangerous for a woman to be driving around a city alone in the middle of the night?"

Prior to her panic a minute ago, she hadn't

even questioned it. Maybe she should have. But that was the trusting part of her. The part that didn't include the male species and wanted to see pretty things instead of danger. She wasn't a complete lunatic and understood the world to be a dangerous place, but when it came to her creative process, certain things, like possible danger, couldn't get in her way. "I live ten minutes from here."

"A lot can happen in ten minutes."

Time to get back to work. Arguing with stubborn people never accomplished much. This, she knew. She resumed drawing a roman shade on the kitchen window. Tangerine would work beautifully.

Brodey wandered to the island, where her discarded sketches smothered the top. Immediately, she snatched them up, but he set his hand on one, tilted his head one way, then the other. "You drew these?"

"Yes, but they're my discards."

"They're pretty good to be discards."

"That's nice of you to say, but trust me, they're discards."

He pointed at the almost-complete sketch on her pad. "That one looks great."

"Thank you. I was stuck on which colors to use. Sometimes when I put it on paper it helps me work it out. When the sun lit this room—"

she swooped one hand "—it was spectacular. I think I need bursts of tangerine in here."

"Uh, okay."

Lexi laughed. "You didn't tell me where your sling was."

"Home. It annoys me. I've been trying to do a few hours each day without it."

"Maybe you should check with your doctor about that?"

"Nah."

As suspected. "Don't tell me you're one of those know-it-all stubborn males."

He gave her one of his cocky grins where one side of his mouth quirked, and she immediately wanted to draw it. "Don't call me stubborn."

Once again, that smile, a little devilish, a little charming and a whole lot irresistible, turned her liquid. It had been months since she'd had even a remote interest in a man. Finding your so-called soul mate sprawled across his desk with another woman tended to do that to a girl. Made her a little less inclined to trust males in general and a whole lot more inclined to demand absolute honesty. No secrets. At all.

And now, tough guy Brodey Hayward had released her smothered sexual desire. On the bright side, at least she wasn't a dead loss and still felt *something*. Even if it was only lust. "What are you doing here so early?"

He held up the envelope. "My dad got me copies of crime-scene notes. I wasn't sure if you worked on Saturdays, but figured I'd get here early and get out of your way. Who knew you'd be here at the crack of dawn?"

"You rolled out of bed this early so you didn't mess up my schedule?"

He shrugged. "You compromised with me yesterday. I owed you one."

All that female desire inside her whipped into a frenzy and she damn near needed a cold shower. "Please tell me you're single because I could kiss you smack on the lips."

"I am most definitely single."

She snorted, then waved him off. So much for her hoping to make him blush. Huh. How she loved a man participating in a little verbal swordplay. "Brodey Hayward, I think I like you." She gestured to the laundry room. "I don't need to be in there yet, so help yourself. I can work around you for an hour or so."

He held up the file. "Thanks. I read the detective's notes, but I need to see the room. Something isn't right."

"Why?"

"I don't have the photos yet. Can't picture the scene. If I set it up, it'll make sense. Want to be my dead body?"

Ew. "Are you kidding?"

"Actually, I'm not. I brought tape, but it'll help if I could see an actual body. All I need is for you to lie on the floor."

She glanced at the sketch desperately waiting for her attention.

He held up his hand. "It'll take five minutes. Promise."

"Five minutes?"

"That's all. I need a visual."

A visual. Considering her early-dawn sketching, she could relate. "Fine. But only because I understand about visuals."

"And, uh, after you play the dead guy, I'll take your place on the floor and maybe you could sketch it for me?"

A frustrated laugh burst free. This man. "What happened to five minutes?"

He grinned. "That's just for lying on the floor. The sketching is separate. Look at it this way. The faster I know what the scene looked like, the sooner I form opinions and hand this thing over to my sister. Then I'm out of here and you're free to do your thing."

Now this boy was talking. And good for him for being intellectually competent enough to figure out how to motivate her.

"If I sketch and lie on the floor, you'll let me get to work in there? Including tearing up that tile?"

"Assuming we don't discover evidence that needs to be collected, yes."

Lexi sighed.

"Hey, I know," he said. "But I won't promise that until I know what I'm dealing with. At the very least, it'd be irresponsible."

For that, she'd give him credit. Some men would lie simply to get their way. Like her cheating ex. *Not going there.* Thinking about him only aggravated her.

She tore her sketch off the pad, set it aside and grabbed her chalk and a pencil. "I have a house to dismantle. Let's get to work."

BRODEY WATCHED OVER Lexi's shoulder as she finished her sketch, and the faint smell of her shampoo, something minty, he thought, like spearmint but not really, worked its way into his system and—look out now—relaxed him. He liked it.

Maybe too much.

She angled back, looking up with those greenish-brown eyes, and something in his brain snapped. Something being the male side of him that hadn't seen any action from a female in a couple of months. Sure there were women he could call, but with the damned arm in a sling, everything—sex included—was way too much work. And it scared the hell out of him because how many men didn't want sex? None that he knew.

Whatever. Mind snap.

"Are you paying attention?" Lexi asked.

More than you know...

"Yeah. I'm thinking." He brought one arm around her so he could point at the sketch and brushed her shoulder along the way. Immediately, he regretted it. Even that meaningless interaction brought his body—very male body—into the red zone. Only thing to do here would be to put his growing erection out of his mind. Maybe today would be the one time that trick worked, but not likely. Considering it had never worked before. "The body needs to be closer to the door."

"Well, Brodey, this is not to scale. You have to allow for some wiggle room."

"I know. It still needs to be closer."

She flipped her pencil to the eraser side and scrubbed it across the paper. A minute later, she'd busted off the outline of the body in the exact place he wanted. "Perfect," he said. "You know, you're really good at this. You should work for the PD."

"No. Thank you, though. What was he wearing that night?"

"Black pants."

She filled in some shading to reflect the slacks the victim wore. "That's better."

"Why not?"

She glanced over her shoulder at him, her perfect lips slightly puckered, her eyes zeroed in as if she'd read his every X-rated thought. Only the hum from the furnace below could be heard in the quiet house, and Brodey's pulse knocked harder. All he had to do was bend down a few inches and those perfect lush lips would be his.

"Wow," he said.

She stepped away, putting distance between them. "It wouldn't work for me. I generally don't sketch people. I do furniture. Furniture is easy. Even if I had the level of skill it requires, I'm not sure I could handle that type of work. I have a friend whose mom was a sketch artist, and it's emotionally draining. What you do—a homicide detective—is a gift. Whether you realize it or not, the average citizen couldn't face the horrors you see every day. I'm one of those people. I like serenity and homey environments. It's what I'm good at."

Good observation since he was already counting down the years—fourteen and a half—until he reached retirement. Not that he didn't have a passion for the job, a passion for righting a wrong, a passion for justice. That justice was what got him out of bed every morning, but studying mangled bodies for thirty years, like some of the guys on the job, didn't seem like a banner way to stay sane. Twenty years would be plenty. Like his dad.

After shading the body, Lexi scratched her cheek, leaving a dark smudge trailing down her face, and he itched to run his fingers across the spot, over the delicate curve of her jaw, and wipe it away. Just to put his hands on her.

She held the sketch out. "What do you think?"

I'd like to tell you what I think. Back to business here. He took the sketch. "It's good. Let's put it on the floor so I can look at."

"Okay. You're all set, then? You don't need me?"

And, hell, if she wasn't the cutest damn thing with that smudge on her cheek. "I'm all set. Except…" Against his better judgment—considering his partial erection might go full-blown—he gently ran the pad of his thumb where the remnants of her sketching marred her creamy skin. Major mistake because now his body went haywire, every nerve snapping.

More.

That was what he wanted. More of her skin under his hands.

She didn't flinch, but locked her gaze on his, and the message was clear. She knew what he wanted. And she wasn't running.

"Smudge?"

"Yep."

"I do that all the time. You'd think I'd learn by now. Thanks for telling me. I'd have been walking around like that."

"No problem," he said. "If touching a beautiful woman's face is the worst thing I do today, I'd say I hit the jackpot."

For a good twenty seconds, she stood in silence, clearly deciding whether to take the bait. *Come on, Lexi, let's play.* But, nope. She broke eye contact and headed to the kitchen, where she'd left her sketches. She turned back to him, casually leaning against the island, but her folded arms and fingers digging into the sleeves of her sweater screamed confusion.

"You know," she said, "you're quite charming when you want to be. I like that about you."

Charming. He'd take it. There were a lot of things he liked about her, too—her confidence, her skill, her ability to shut down an uncomfortable conversation without making a big deal about it. The woman had a way about her.

"I do try."

She nodded toward the laundry room. "How long until you're finished?"

"I don't know yet. I'll read the ME's report and the crime-scene notes again. The angle of the body is weird." He shifted in the doorway.

"Unless he was standing like this, facing the wall. Or maybe the killer moved the body. I don't know. I need to study it."

"So, what you're telling me is I won't be able to get into this room again today?"

Here we go again. All that light banter from twenty seconds ago? Gone. Vanished. Vamoosed. "Lexi, I don't know. Trust me, I'd love to tell you it'll be today. It might be. I need to study these notes more. Sorry if it's ripping into your forty-five days, but the guy is dead."

"Oh, don't even go there. Do *not* try to make me feel like I'm being unreasonable for wanting to get this project done. I have been nothing but cooperative. I want to give this woman peace as much as anyone. Part of that will come from unloading this house before she's forced into bankruptcy. So, spare me your lecture." She scooped up her pad and shoved the loose sketches into it. "Call me when you're through holding up my work."

Great. Mad. How the hell had this become his fault? He moved to the island, where she'd already left skid marks on her way to the front door, and held his arms wide. For once, the elbow didn't holler, but the gesture was useless since she couldn't see him. Well, fine. His whole point of getting here early was to work alone. All she did was distract him. Between her looks and the way she smelled, his body responded to her. Couple that with her insistence that he rush through his investigation, and Alexis Vanderbilt snatched his energy. Just sucked him dry.

The front door slammed and he shook his head, pondering whether or not to chase after her. *Let her go.* He'd get more done without her.

Even if she smelled good.

LEXI TROMPED DOWN the Williamses' walkway, sketch pad in hand, coat flapping and the wrath of a winter day descending on anyone fool enough to venture outside. Mere breathing brought the wind—frigid, bone-shattering wind—burning down her throat.

"I need to be a snowbird," she muttered.

"Morning."

She halted a second before slamming into a man walking his Yorkie. "Oh, I'm sorry. I wasn't paying attention."

"I see that."

The man wore a long wool coat over a suit. His close-cropped, graying hair gave him an edge of sophistication that topped off the whole "I have money" vibe. By the looks of him and the adorable dog, he was a neighbor. He held a mug in one hand, and the aroma of hazelnut reminded Lexi she hadn't put anything into her system in nearly twelve hours. On the way home, she'd stop at the coffee shop and load up on caffeine and sugar. A chocolate croissant might do the trick. The man eyed her, then glanced back at the house. "Are you the real-estate agent?"

On the surface, the question seemed harmless, but Lexi had worked with enough gossip-mongers to know her words could storm this community. "No. Not the real-estate agent."

"Ah. The designer, then." Mug in hand, he gestured down the block. "Phillips. We live two doors down. We heard Brenda hired someone to stage the house. It's a rotten situation."

The gossip trail. How she despised it. "It is indeed."

But wait. He was a neighbor, presumably questioned by the police. Perhaps he saw or heard something that could help Brodey's investigation along.

And get her back on schedule.

"Mr. Phillips, were you home the night Mr. Williams died?"

The tiny Yorkie nudged the leash and Phillips took three steps closer to the tree. "I was. The police talked to my wife and me."

"Did you see anyone?"

"No. Didn't hear anything, either. With the increased security, we're usually aware of problems, but it was quiet that night. Perplexing."

Perplexing. Interesting word choice. And the cadence, so direct, pegged him as a lawyer or maybe an executive with a lot of authority.

"I see. Thank you."

"Of course. When your work is complete, do you mind if my wife and I take a look? She wants to redo the kitchen."

Lexi smiled. Crabby and dressed like a coed but somehow she might gain a client from this. "That would be up to Mrs. Williams, but I'd be happy to ask her if you'd like."

"I'd appreciate that. Thanks."

Once tucked into her car, Lexi jotted Mr. Phillips's address and a note to herself to ask Brenda about him. Maybe she'd even be nice and share her conversation with Brodey. *Maybe.* For now, she needed food and a shower before her appointment in Lincoln Park. A quasi-appointment. Her college roommate, thanks to her new job as an on-air anchor for a local cable news station, had finally taken the plunge and bought a house. If it could be called a house. Sucked from the clutches of foreclosure, the three-story monstrosity needed loads of work.

Candace had recruited Lexi to help.

Ninety minutes later, Lexi knocked on Candace's front door, where the knocker promptly fell off in her hand.

The door swung open. "Hi, doll." Candace

spotted the detached door knocker and plucked it from Lexi's hand. "I forgot to warn you about that. I have a new one. I just don't know how to install it."

"I can do it. Do you have a drill?"

"You're kidding, right?"

Lexi laughed. "About me installing it or the drill?"

"The drill. You can do anything. Everyone knows that."

"I love when you suck up."

She swept her arm in a huge semicircle. "Welcome to paradise."

Lexi glanced around the foyer, where fist-size holes marred the walls. Someone had done a number on the place. "If this is paradise, I want out."

"I know. The old owners ripped every light fixture out. They even took the copper pipes. The place is an eyesore, but your very own Nate said it's structurally sound. Don't worry. All the mold has been removed."

Mold. Dear God. "Excellent."

"Thank you for squeezing me in."

"It's fine. I'm working on another project that suddenly has a delay. A delay by way of a hunky detective."

Being a single and clock-ticking female, Candace pursed her lips. "Hunky detectives?"

"One hunky detective. Not plural."

Candace rolled her bottom lip in disappointment and Lexi raised her hands. "Don't stress. The way things are going, he and I don't exactly agree, so he might be yours by default."

"What happened?"

"It's the Williams project. Brodey is on short-term disability leave—elbow surgery—from the police department. He's a homicide detective."

"Ew."

"Exactly. Anyway, his sister, Jenna, is a private investigator Mrs. Williams hired to look into her husband's murder. Jenna recruited him to help. The man is bored and has thrown himself into this. At this moment, he's coming up with all the reasons I can't demolish the laundry room."

Candace folded her arms and leaned against a railing that looked barely stable enough to support its own weight, never mind hers. "And that's killing your forty-five-day timeline."

"Yes. Thank you! The hunky detective doesn't seem to understand that I need to get this house sold. I want that bonus. The bonus gets me my assistant, a solid seven hours of sleep every night and time to clean out my garage so I can make it an office. I'm ready to collapse."

"I can't believe you haven't cleaned that mess out. Hire someone to do it, for God's sake."

"No. There's a ton of stuff in there from the old owner. There might be lost treasures I can use."

Candace waved her to the kitchen. "I have a fresh pot on. You need to decompress for a few minutes before we get into this."

That sounded heavenly. Decompression. With a pal. Realization hit that she'd spent the past months virtually ignoring her friends. "I'm sorry."

"For what?"

"For being a bad friend."

"Honey, you're helping me with this pit and not charging me. You're a great friend."

"That's not what I mean. I've been busy and haven't made time for the people I care about. That's not right."

"So, you help sell the Williams place and hire an assistant. You're fixing it. Don't be hard on yourself because you're ambitious. Now, back to more important matters. What's up with this hunk? Has he discovered anything on the murder?"

They entered the kitchen, and the aroma of freshly brewed coffee taunted Lexi's senses. The surprisingly clean maple cabinets glowed, but the peeling linoleum counters had to go. The cabinets could probably stay, but not the linoleum. Candace filled two mugs and set one down next to the cream and sugar so Lexi could destroy a perfect cup of black coffee. Her friends knew her so well.

"He just started. Heck, I'm even helping him. On the way out of the house this morning I met one of the neighbors walking his dog. He stopped me. Being nosy, I guess. Anyway, I asked him if he saw anything the night of the murder."

"And?"

She dumped two teaspoons of sugar into her coffee, poured milk in and took a gulp. "Nada. Of course, I don't know what I expected. I just want this thing wrapped up so I can get to work."

Candace set her cup on the island and leaned on her elbows. "I've been following this story for work. It's amazing that in such a tight community they have no leads. Someone had to have seen something."

"You'd think. Maybe talking to the police scares them."

"What does your hunky detective think?"

"He thinks there's evidence in the laundry room and won't let me rip it up. We had a blowout about it this morning."

Candace tilted her head and narrowed her eyes in that determined-reporter way of hers. "You like this guy."

Unfortunately, yes. "You haven't seen him.

There's plenty to like. Setting aside that whole pushy-alpha-male thing. Honestly, he's a little annoying."

"And, yet, you like him. Which, correct me if I'm wrong, is a big step for you. You haven't been interested in a man since—"

Lexi's arms shot up. "Whoa, girlfriend. I know exactly how long it's been. We don't need to discuss it."

Candace waved her off. "What are you doing about this blowout with the detective? Come on, Lex, I can tell you like this guy. It sounds like he's just trying to do his job—even if it is a volunteer assignment." She leaned in, gave Lexi a wicked smile. "How often do hunky detectives come into your life?"

Not very often. In fact, there hadn't been an onslaught of hunky men in her life at all lately. But the stubborn part of her didn't want to give in and admit she was wrong.

Coffee sloshed in her stomach, letting her know that maybe the chocolate croissant hadn't settled so well. Since she'd walked out on Brodey, she'd felt like this. Nauseated. Uneasy. Off-kilter. And she hadn't felt any of those things in a very long time.

She shook her head. "I'm not wrong for wanting to do my job."

"I didn't say you were. I think this is one of

those situations where you're both right and simply can't agree. All I'm saying is maybe you need to look at it from his side, too."

Candace came around the island, dropped her arm over Lexi's shoulder and gave her a squeeze. "Honey, I think it's time you let yourself like men again. And this detective sounds like he might be a great start."

Chapter Six

By 3:00 p.m. Brodey made his second trip of the day to the Williams place. Bit by bit, more information streamed in from detectives who owed his old man favors. The latest was a detailed evidence list, including descriptions of a slug that had been pulled from the wall in the laundry room. Apparently, one shot missed its target. By now the wall would have been repaired, but he might as well satisfy his curiosity and have a look.

Crime-scene photos would help. They'd show the blood spatter that often told the story of who was standing where when life got ugly.

Biting wind ripped into him and he dipped his head lower, huddling into his jacket. Even with his hatred of winter coats, he wouldn't tackle a three-block walk in these temps without one. So far today he'd managed four hours without the sling. After his blowout with Lexi that morning, he'd gone home and sacked out for two hours.

Between sleep and the afternoon back in the sling, he was good to go again.

At the corner of the Williamses' block, he hooked a right and—hello—found his sister and one extremely hot blonde, otherwise known as Lexi, standing in front of a tree. What were they up to?

Lexi handed a piece of paper to Jenna, who held it up to the tree, ramming it home with a staple gun. "Ladies," he called, "what the hell are you doing?"

After one last staple, they both turned. "Hey," Jenna said. "What are you doing here?"

Still approaching, he held up his suddenly ever-present file. "Dad got me an evidence list. Getting a look at the wall where they pulled a slug."

"Nice," she said. "We're almost done here and I'll join you."

He stopped in front of the tree and studied the paper. The one with a photo of their vic and a phone number to call with information. Silently, he read off the number, but didn't recognize it.

"Brodey," his sister said, "don't even try it. It's a good idea. And it certainly can't hurt."

"You want to crack a cold case by posting flyers?"

"Yes," Lexi said. "She does."

Great. Now they were a team. "Lexi," he said, "how'd you get involved in this?"

"I was heading to the house to try out samples and spotted Jenna posting the flyers." She grinned. "I'm the helper."

Jenna waved the staple gun at him. "And before you start in, I called Brenda this morning and talked to her about it. Her only concern was the kids seeing them, but since she doesn't bring the kids here anymore she said it's okay."

"And, frankly," Lexi said, "this case is stalled. Someone around here must have seen something. Maybe the police accidentally missed something. Who knows?"

Jenna went back to stapling. "You know people talk to me, Brodey. It'll be fine."

No doubt they would talk to her. One thing about his baby sister, men saw her coming and a different part of their anatomy took over. She knew that. Had used it to her advantage many times, but this? This was insanity. "Jenna, why don't you just write your number on a prison wall? Do you have any idea how dangerous this is?"

That got him an eye roll. "Relax, it's a disposable phone. When we're done, I'll get rid of it. You know, it wouldn't kill you to give me a little credit. Between my law-enforcement father and my US marshal boyfriend, I've learned a few things."

"Yeah, well, how about putting what you've learned to use and not setting yourself up to be attacked?"

Jenna poked the staple gun at him. "You're out of line."

Brodey flapped his hand at her. "Quit waving that thing around. I don't like you two wandering around handing out flyers. Anyway, in this neighborhood there's probably an ordinance prohibiting posting them."

"Got that covered, big brother. Brenda called the security people and cleared it."

"Right," Lexi snarked. "One of their residents is dead. They want this solved as much as we do. Leave her alone. She knows what she's doing."

Like his sister, Lexi had an answer for everything. His chances of coming out on top here were zip. A smart man knew when to run like hell, and his mama never accused him of being stupid. He'd try a different approach. The scary-as-hell one. "You two do whatever you want, but I'd appreciate it if you tried not to get killed." He angled around them and headed for the house. "I'll be inside. Call me if you need me."

A few seconds later, a solo Jenna ran up beside him, her heels clicking against the concrete. For probably the thousandth time, he marveled over how women ran in high-heeled boots. "Where's Lexi?"

"Back at her car grabbing carpet samples."

He stopped, shifted sideways and spotted her popping the trunk on a vehicle not half a block away.

"Brodey, she'll be fine. I have never met such a worrywart."

"It never hurts to be cautious."

"Cautious is one thing, paranoid is another."

"I'm not paranoid." *Yeah, I am.* "Maybe I'm a little paranoid, but with what I do for a living, I think that's normal."

Jenna snorted. "You're funny."

Leaving him on the sidewalk, she dug out the key to the Williams home and unlocked the front door. Once again, he glanced back, making sure Lexi was squared away. Still down the block, she shut her trunk, checked that it had latched and hefted a bag over her shoulder.

That bag looked pretty damned heavy. He started back down the block toward her. "Sit tight. I'll help you."

"I've got it!"

Of course. He liked independent women, but could they accept some help every now and again? "You sure?"

"Yes." Four cars down she hesitated, stared

down at the few samples in her hands. "Shoot. I forgot one in the car. I'll meet you inside."

He stood for a minute, waiting. Another few minutes wouldn't matter. Once she got back, they'd go inside together.

"Brodey," Jenna said from the open doorway, "she's fine. Can we do this? Mr. Hennings called me an hour ago with a lead on a case that's *not* pro bono, and I need to get moving on it."

For another few seconds, he watched Lexi head back to her car, pop the trunk and mess around in there. "You good?" he hollered.

She slammed the trunk and held up her hand.

"I'm going in," Jenna said. "Hurry up and stop obsessing."

Ha. He'd never stop obsessing and she knew it. Doing what he did for a living, he saw things that horrified and shocked him on a daily basis. Maintaining his sanity meant locking up the bad guys and reducing the depravity.

Lexi might be only half a block away, but a lot could happen in that half a block. Rape, abduction, wayward bullet. None of it would surprise him. He glanced up and down the block, saw nothing suspicious, then checked on Lexi finally making her way back to him. In another minute she'd be walking into the house. "Go inside!" she hollered. "I'm fine. I'll be right there."

"Okay," he muttered. She had only a short

distance to go. Plus, his sister was in a rush and he didn't want to hear her griping. He turned and marched up the steps. "Let's see if we can find this bullet hole."

LEXI HEFTED THE bag of carpet samples and hoped she hadn't forgotten anything else because it was darned cold and her toes were blocks of ice. She beelined for the warmth of the house, determined to get this thing staged and sold by her deadline. Even if it destroyed her.

With Brodey traipsing around, it just might. The man created all sorts of interruptions. Before he stormed into her life, she hadn't missed the simplicity of a physical connection. Now, between fantasizing about him touching her, his overprotectiveness and his pain-in-the-butt way of trying to control every situation, she wasn't sure if she wanted to kill him or curl into a warm bed with him. Although, either choice might work. For a fling. At this point, she had no interest in falling in love, but maybe Candace was right and she needed to lighten up. At least a little. If only she could unsee that pig of an ex stretched across his desk with the twenty-year-old.

Crash. Her shoulder connected with something—definitely bigger—and she wobbled sideways. A man caught her arm and kept her from going over, but her bag of samples tumbled to the ground.

How many times would she plow into strange men before she started paying attention? She bolted upright, attempting to balance herself as he gripped her arm. "I'm so sorry," she said.

"No. My fault. I wasn't paying attention. Are you hurt?"

His voice had a rawness to it, a weird rasp that made her think of singed vocal cords. "Oh, heavens no. I'm fine."

She shrugged free of his too-tight grasp and adjusted her coat sleeves. He wore a down jacket with a ripped left sleeve and a pair of ratty, faded jeans. The shredded hems must have been dragged across pavement as he walked. She raised her head and took in his face—day-old beard, crisp blue eyes and untrimmed hair that dipped well below his earlobes. His cheekbones cut severely into a slope to his pointy chin, giving him a cartoonish appearance. Distinctive features.

His nearness kicked up a dull throb in her stomach. The man looked harmless, if a bit messy, but that stomach thing didn't happen often and she'd take it as a message to move on.

She stepped back, reached for her sample bag and glanced at the Williams home, where

Brodey no longer stood on the sidewalk. "Thank you for keeping me upright."

"I've seen you in the neighborhood," the man said.

She backed up another step. *Come on, Brodey. Come back outside.*

When she didn't respond, he gestured with his chin to the opposite end of the block. "I live down the street. You're doing work on the Williams place, right?"

The pinnacle of rudeness would be to simply walk away. That she wouldn't do. With her luck, he'd be an eccentric billionaire hunting for a designer and he'd tell every one of his rich friends she blew him off.

No blowing him off.

Faking it the whole way, she smiled and pointed to the home. "I'm the interior designer. I'm sorry, though, I have people waiting for me."

Letting him know she wasn't alone couldn't hurt.

"Sure," he said. "But if I'm in the market for a designer, how should I get hold of you?"

Normally, she'd whip out a business card, but not this time. Compared with meeting the man with the Yorkie earlier, something about this encounter didn't fit. She patted her pockets, then riffled through her purse. Her hand landed on her wallet, where she stored her business cards in the outer pocket, but she continued feeling around. "Well, shoot. I forgot my cards, but I'll be working here for a while. If you'd like, leave a note on the door with your phone number and I'll call you."

He tilted his head one way, then the other, those icy blue eyes on her in a way that wasn't quite sexual, but definitely wasn't innocent, either. Lexi's stomach twisted. An absolute clue to leave if there ever was one. "Thank you again."

She moved away, pulling out her phone as she marched down the street. She glanced behind her. The man continued to watch her and she picked up her pace, tripping on a raised edge of sidewalk. Ouch! Toe throbbing, she stumbled three steps and almost, once again, hit the ground. Finally, she caught her balance and checked behind her. The man turned in the opposite direction, the direction he said he lived, and hunched into the wind, walking away from her.

Probably a false alarm. Or Brodey's paranoia rubbing off. She grunted and hurried up the steps. Inside the house, she set her bag on the dirty-snow carpet, squatted and began organizing her samples. She'd love to do a hand-scraped walnut in here. If the budget didn't allow it, she'd find something cheaper, but the room begged for hardwood.

Something poked her shoulder and she flinched, the movement knocking her off balance enough that she toppled to her rear. After the first two saves so far today, this time she couldn't keep herself upright. *So elegant.*

"Whoa," Brodey said. "You okay? What took you so long?"

He held out both hands and she grasped them, letting him boost her up. In contrast to those of the man outside, Brodey's hands were warm and gentle and steady and nothing, not one thing, about them made her uneasy. Exactly how it should be. "I'm…fine."

"You don't sound fine."

"Brodey, I'm fine. I need to go through these samples, though."

"Who was that guy you were talking to?"

He'd seen. *Grrr…*

"I don't know. He said he was a neighbor. I wasn't paying attention and bumped into him."

He tilted his head, studied her face. "Did he say something?"

"No. Why?"

"Because before you talked to him you were smarting off and relaxed. Now you're like a trip wire. What did he say?"

Damned perceptive man. Considering his job, she shouldn't have expected any different.

Squatting again, she lined up two more samples. "It wasn't what he said so much."

"What, then?"

She shrugged. "He knew I was working here. And his clothes. This morning I met a neighbor and—" she circled one hand "—well, he *fit*. Everything about him screamed affluence. The guy just now, not so much. Ripped jacket, torn jeans and an overall messy look. But I could be wrong."

He grabbed her notepad and pen from her briefcase and shoved them at her. "Lex, do not minimize what you are feeling here. That's your first mistake. Sketch him. Before you lose the details."

"Brodey—"

"I want the details before you forget. Please. Humor me?"

And oh, that look in his eyes. Soft and pleading and so darned beautiful. Totally playing her and she didn't care. So what? A little caution couldn't hurt. She dug in her purse for a pencil. "I can't use a pen."

Dropping to a sitting position on the carpet, she roughed out a sketch—the sloping cheekbones, the pointy chin and messy hair. "His eyes were a weird blue. Icy blue."

"What's up?" Jenna asked from the hallway leading to the kitchen.

"Shh."

Brodey remained quiet as the minutes ticked by and Lexi finished her sketch. Not perfect, but enough.

"That's good. Did he say where he lives?"

"Not specifically. He said down the street. South end of the block."

He nodded, tore her sketch from the pad and hopped to his feet. "Wait here. I'll be right back. Do *not* leave this house. Either of you."

Jenna sighed. "Where are you going?"

He held up the sketch. "To find this guy."

BRODEY KNOCKED ON the neighbor's door, automatically reaching for his badge that wasn't there. Another thing he hated about disability leave. Giving up his gun and creds. He'd work around it. The door opened and a middle-aged woman, smartly dressed in gray slacks, a black turtleneck and a string of pearls, greeted him. If this was her hanging-around-the-house look, she needed to ease up.

"Can I help you?"

"Yes, ma'am. I'm Detective Brodey Hayward. I'm looking into the Williams murder."

Probably, he shouldn't have added *detective* to his name. Call it habit, call it adrenaline zapping his good sense, call it whatever, but he was in it now and if this woman was smart, she'd question his lack of badge, shut the door and call the PD to verify what he'd told her. If it got back to his boss, he'd be cooked. But he couldn't worry about it now after every alarm bell—the skittering pulse, the tickle at the base of his neck, the sweating on a blistering-cold day—went off.

"I see," she said. "I hope they find who did it soon. It's completely unnerving."

"Yes, ma'am." He held out the sketch. "Would you mind taking a look at this? Do you recognize this man?"

Shivering against the wind, she glanced down and puckered her lips. Her eyebrows squeezed in and the no-clue look told him everything he needed to know. She didn't know him. And with a neighborhood this tight, she'd know him.

"I can't say that I recognize him. Should I? Is he a suspect?"

"We're looking into several persons of interest."

She shrugged and handed him the sketch back. "I'm sorry. I don't recognize him."

"Thank you. I appreciate it."

Next house. In fact, he'd hit every house on the block until he found this guy. Even as a beat cop he never minded canvassing a neighborhood. He got off on the lure of detective work, questioning people, searching for that one element that might crack a case.

Canvassing on a fall or summer day was a whole lot more fun, but he'd keep moving and get body heat going. He zipped his jacket, stepped off the porch and trekked on.

Three houses later, no one recognized the sketch. Which meant Lexi had either heard something incorrectly and the guy didn't live on this block or he'd lied. Lexi, with her attention to detail, wouldn't screw something like this up, and with the guy's banged-up appearance, it was more likely he'd lied. Brodey pulled out his phone and scrolled to the number Lexi had given him before their meeting with Brenda the day before.

"Hi," she said. "Where are you?"

"Canvassing. Are you sure he said he lived on this block?"

"Yes."

"You're sure?"

"Positive. He said he lived 'down the street.' Those were his exact words. I took that to mean he lived on the block. Why?"

Okay, he'd buy that. "Because I've been to three houses and no one recognizes him. In a neighborhood like this, they know who lives on their street. I'll finish the rest of the block and if I can't find him, I'm going to security. They'll know everyone here. If they don't, then we need to figure out who this is and why he knew you were working at the Williams place."

Brodey ended the call and continued the search. After hitting every house on the block and visiting the security guard cruising the block in an SUV, he returned to the house, where Jenna tore out of the kitchen mumbling various swearwords. Apparently, he'd made her late. But, hell, they were investigating a damned murder.

She stuffed her arms into her coat and buttoned it with the speed of a sprinter. "Did you find him?"

"No."

Behind her, heels clicked against tile in rapid-fire tap-tap-taps and Lexi swung into the hallway. He watched and let his gaze move up her legs, and immediately his temperature shot up. "Security doesn't know him and no one I talked to does, either. I'd say your assessment that he doesn't fit here is correct."

For a few seconds, she stood stock-still, only her throat moving as she swallowed once, then a second time. "Could he have been a thief casing the neighborhood?"

Brodey clucked his tongue. "Maybe. But if he is, he's one of the worst ever. Why would he approach you and ask if you were working here? No thief does that."

"Okay, kids," Jenna said. "I'm sorry, but I have a lead to chase before my boss gets mad at me. Can you guys handle this?"

"You're dumping this on us? After you brought me in on it?"

Jenna tugged his sleeve and planted a kiss on his cheek. "I know. I'm sorry. This other case is a real heater, though, and you know that means Gerald Hennings will be all over the news. Likely with information I've provided, so I'd better get to it and be right about whatever I tell him. I'll call you later. Let me know what I can do to help you find this guy."

"I will. Be careful. And, as much as the pair of you call me paranoid, he probably saw two beautiful women posting flyers and was either up to no good or hitting on you. If he was hitting on you, his technique stinks."

Lexi sighed. Too bad. She'd have to endure it because that guy tripped every one of Brodey's alerts.

Jenna waved both arms at him. "I'm leaving before I throw something at you. Call me later."

She flew out the door, once again leaving Brodey alone with Lexi. Not altogether a horrible situation.

"So," Lexi said, "you think he intended to attack one of us?"

"That or he saw you two posting flyers and wanted to pump you for information about the case. Maybe he knows something. *Maybe* he's involved."

"Oh no."

Using her right hand, she grabbed the index finger of her left hand, fiddling with it, pressing on her nail, then slowly moving to the next one. Nervous habit. When she spotted him watching, she dropped her hands, let her arms hang at her sides.

"Precisely why I reamed you two for the flyer stunt. Not only does the guy know you're working here, sometimes alone—which has to stop—but now he has my sister's phone number. Lexi, seriously, you cannot be here alone. This guy might have nothing to do with the Williams murder, but whoever he is, he shouldn't have been here. At the very least, he's probably a thief. And we don't want to consider what he could be at his worst."

She propped her hands on her hips and blew out a breath. At any second, she would, as his sister always did, accuse him of being paranoid or cynical. Cynical until a murderer carved someone to pieces and shoved the body into a trunk. "Whatever argument you're planning, forget it. It won't work. I'm dug in."

"I wasn't going to argue."

Sure she wasn't. He snorted.

She touched his arm, gently pressing her fingers against his sleeve. Not hard, but enough to get his attention. "I was thinking about how having someone here with me constantly would slow me down."

"Better slow than dead."

"I get it, Brodey. Relax."

He'd never relax. That was half his problem. Always watching—and waiting—for what could go wrong. Where Lexi saw possibilities, he saw problems. How many times had he gotten in trouble with dates because he couldn't sit through a meal at a restaurant without constantly scanning the place? The force of that, the final acceptance that his quest to keep people safe had turned into a daily pummeling over the world being a hideous place, set him back a step, literally pushing him.

"What's wrong?"

He scrubbed his good hand over his face, focused on his pounding heart and breathed in. "I don't know. No. That's a lie. I do know. My job is important. I know I make a difference. But I see the world from a cop's eyes. Every damned day, I'm scanning, searching for what might go wrong. Maybe I am paranoid."

She moved closer, close enough that the energy around him charged his already amped system and…yeah…he needed to blow off some steam.

In ways he couldn't admit right now.

"You're overly cautious," she said. "It's not a bad thing. With what you do for a living, I'd think it's natural. But give yourself a break." She tugged on his shirt, inched just a little closer and grinned. "Enjoy the fact that you were right. I don't intend on letting that happen a lot."

Holy hell, all that crackling energy fried him. Parts of the southern end of his body went rock hard.

"Lex?"

Her gaze moved to his lips. "Yes?"

"You might want to step back."

"I might." She looked up, locked eyes with him. "Or I might not."

That right there would be what his boss called a go sign. A giant one. He dipped his head lower, testing, anticipating her reaction. In response, she tilted hers up.

Definite go sign.

Before he analyzed this thing too much, he slid his good arm around her waist, sunk his fingers into the warm, soft flesh under her blouse.

He needed this woman. No doubt. He kissed her. At first gently—and man oh man—better than he thought. She boosted up on her toes, slipped her arms around his neck, pressing her body dead against him, and if he didn't have this damned sling on, he'd have mauled her. Just clamped his fingers over her rear, dragged her even closer and feasted on her.

Possibly reading his mind, she drove her tongue into his mouth and—*thank you, thank you*—it appeared a man didn't have to die to get the express train to heaven. He pulled her hips closer, let her feel just how much his body craved her, and a small noise came from her throat.

Yeah, honey, that's what you do to me.

He was coming apart and losing his damned mind.

Here he was, standing in the foyer of a murder victim's house, sucking the hell out of the decorator. What was wrong with him? The fact that he hadn't gotten any action in a few months might be a clue.

Another noise filled the empty house. A clanging and it wasn't his imagination.

Lexi pulled back. "Just shoot me."

"Not on your life. What's that banging?"

"The alarm on my phone."

"Why?"

"I have an appointment in fifteen minutes."

Come on. Really? Now?

She backed up two more steps, as if to level the death blow, the seriously hurtful this-is-not-happening one.

"I'm sorry," she said. "Can we pick this up later?"

No. *Forget the appointment.* Not fair. Not for one second. But then he imagined the roles being reversed, imagined he'd caught a case. Her job might not include getting called to a crime scene, but she had responsibilities. To her clients and to herself.

Which blew things for him.

He ran the back of his hand along her cheek, the heat there not escaping him. "Sure," he said. "Later is good."

Hopefully, really good.

AFTER HER APPOINTMENT, a consultation with a doctor and his wife who lived in a Gold Coast high-rise, Lexi treated herself to Thai. Strong buying signals from the doctor's wife deserved a celebration. If she landed that job, there were plenty of other residents in the building who undoubtedly, based on their location, could afford to hire her.

Yes, sirree, that assistant was in striking range. After dinner, she'd go through the growing stack of résumés she'd received and see if there were more possible candidates. So far, she'd interviewed a handful of applicants and had narrowed it to two possibilities. One being an art and design student from Columbia College. Attending school so close to Lexi's client base was a plus and hopefully, she could grow into being more than an assistant and take on clients of her own. Expansion. What a lovely word.

Continuing on her good-luck streak, Lexi claimed a parking spot half a block from her Bucktown cottage. The short distance allowed for her to make only one trip from the car. If Brodey were here he'd tell her that with her hands full like that, she'd be a prime target for a mugger. Even with Bucktown considered a moderately safe neighborhood, she glanced around, checking behind her and across the street. Total darkness.

Still, she'd made the effort.

Originally named because Polish immigrants raised male goats—aka bucks—there, Bucktown had grown into a community loaded with musicians and artists. While house hunting, she was intrigued by the artsy vibe. She loved this neighborhood. Then she'd seen her cottage and vowed to have it. She'd bought the barely nine-hundred-square-foot cottage from a man whose father had passed. The son lived out West and, given the state of disrepair, couldn't tend to the cottage. Lexi offered to take it off his hands—well below the asking price—and rehab it herself. With the spectacular price came a detached garage.

Full of junk.

At the time, it seemed like a steal. Now, almost two years later, she'd yet to find time to gut the garage and turn it into her dream office.

Turning onto her walkway, she spotted the silhouette of someone—most definitely male—on her bench by the front door, and Brodey's lecturing voice filled her head. She loosened her fingers on her briefcase and bag of Thai, preparing to fling them and run. A cold, relentless pounding in her chest stole her breath, kept it trapped in the center of her throat, paralyzing her.

Run.

"It's me," the man said. "Brodey."

Air came in a whoosh, flooding her oxygen-deprived brain, and she dropped her briefcase and dinner, bent at the waist and breathed. Heaven help her if she passed out.

"Brodey! You scared the daylights out of me."

He stood, barely a shadow moving in the blackness. Typically, the Jansens had their porch lit, but not tonight. Of all nights for the light to be off. That little fact was sure to earn her another lecture from King Paranoid.

"Sorry. But you know—"

She picked up the briefcase. "Save it. I know I should have a light on. Usually the Jansens— my neighbors—have the block lit up."

"At the very least, a motion detector."

In the darkness, she grinned. The man took obsessive to new heights. But after this little episode, that motion detector might not be a bad idea.

She set her briefcase and dinner on the small bench Brodey had just risen from. "It's freezing out here. Let me dig out my key and we'll go inside. And don't nag me about how I should have had the key out. My hands were full and I forgot to grab it before I loaded up. I know I shouldn't have had my hands full."

Good grief. Everything she did around this man was wrong.

"It's for your own good."

She sighed. "This protective streak is nice, but let's not get carried away. How'd you know where I live?"

He gave her a droll look.

"Never mind. Dumb question to ask a homicide detective. Why are you here anyway?"

"I...uh...wanted to apologize if I was hard on you earlier."

She unlocked the door, pushed it open and flipped on the light before waving him in. *Apologize.* Maybe she wasn't *always* wrong. "When?"

He grabbed her dinner and briefcase off the bench and carried it in for her. "When you told me about the neighbor who's not a neighbor."

Ah. That. "Jenna told you to call, didn't she?"

"No."

"I don't believe you."

He smiled, lightning fast and devastating. "Well, maybe she suggested it."

"What did she really say?"

"She said I can be an overbearing ape and I probably owed you an apology."

"Wow."

"Yeah. We don't pull punches in my family."

"I guess not." She took the bag and waved him in. "Dump that briefcase by the door and have a seat."

Doing as he was told, he set the briefcase down, shoved his hands into his pockets and studied the room. He did that a lot. Studied things. Must be the investigator in him.

"This place is something," he said. "Guessing you decorated it."

There was that word again. "Yes, I *designed* it."

Every inch of the mint walls, the camel-colored leather chairs and pops of red on the side tables had been her creation. She breathed in. "This place launched my career."

Brodey dropped onto the sofa and rested his head back. "Oh, man. I want this."

You should, big fella. Considering the twenty-thousand-dollar price tag, he'd better keep his feet off it.

"Amazing, isn't it? I didn't even have to pay for it."

"No kidding?"

"Nope. That was part of my career launch, too. I entered a contest in *Home Design Magazine*. I was in the Small Spaces category and took second place. I still think I got robbed, but whatever. Anyway, I talked Fireside Furniture into sponsoring me and they gave me the sofa. When I made it to the finals, they got great PR out of it and I had a flood of clients from all over the city calling me. It was the proverbial win-win. I love this place."

He cocked his head and met her gaze. "That's...impressive."

"Not bad for a *decorator*, huh?"

He held up his hands. "All right, I've got it. No more decorator cracks."

The kitchen was an extension of the living room, and she placed the Thai on the breakfast bar separating the two areas. "Thank you. The only thing left to do is the garage. As soon as I have time, I'll get it cleaned out and make an office out of it."

Then I'll have a life again.

"There's a garage?"

"Out back by the alley. Have you eaten? I bought Thai."

"Not yet. You go ahead, though."

"I have plenty. I always buy extra for leftovers." She batted her eyes. "I'll share."

He pushed out of the sofa and moved to the kitchen, his eyes still on her and, well, unnerving her way more than she'd like. "Why are you staring at me?"

He jerked one shoulder. "I like to look at you." He pointed to the bag. "Can I help?"

That was his answer? He liked to look at her? As if it was no big deal. As if they hadn't shared that amazing kiss earlier, and now the staring, and what? She wasn't supposed to jump him? Really? A man who looked liked this said something like that and she was supposed to act as if her hormones weren't in a twist. She spun away from him, breaking the eye contact. Otherwise, she'd break something else when she pounced on him. "Park yourself and I'll get dishes. I'm having water to drink. Would you like something else?"

"Water is good. Thanks."

She grabbed two water bottles from the fridge and a couple of glasses from the drying rack and poured. "How did you do with the wall?"

"The slug? Not good. There's nothing there. They replaced the drywall. I don't know what I was looking for anyway."

"Is there something bugging you?"

"I don't know. Probably."

She laughed. Men. Such funny creatures. "From what I know of the case, the original detectives thought it was an intruder who shot Mr. Williams."

"Yeah. They thought someone came in through the laundry room window because it was open."

"You don't believe that?"

"I don't *not* believe it. By the way, the sketch you did for me is almost dead-on to the actual crime scene. You have amazing instincts. Which I guess is why you're so good at what you do. The only thing we missed was the broken glass on the floor. That was in the detective's notes, but you didn't know that."

She smiled. "Instincts help, but I think for me it's more about details. I see things people don't usually see."

He eyed her, his gaze fixed and steady. Thinking. About what, who knew?

"What is it?"

"The glass on the floor."

"What about it? Food is ready."

She set the bowls down, but Brodey sat back in the high-backed stool and stared at the ceiling. "Crime-scene photos showed the open window the intruder came through. The outside entry door was to the left of the window." He gestured sideways with his hands. "The broken glass on the floor."

"Okay. But shouldn't Jenna be doing this? I mean, it is her case."

"Technically, yeah. But she called before and she's knee-deep in this other case. The *paying* client. I told her I'd run with this. See what I came up with."

"You're a good brother."

That got a smile out of him. All crooked and wicked and enough to chip away at the wall of stone around her heart. "I do try. Even when she drives me insane."

Lexi scooted around the counter and took the stool next to him. He could theorize all he wanted, but she hadn't eaten since breakfast and needed fuel.

"The broken glass," he said.

"What about it?"

He reached for one of the glasses. "Stand up."

There goes dinner. Before moving, she shoved

a forkful of noodles into her mouth—how incredibly elegant—and took the glass.

"You be the victim," he said. "I'll be the bad guy. Don't put that glass down yet." He walked to the front door. "Let's say this is the entry and I come in." He stepped outside. A few seconds later, the door flew open and—*whap*—hit the wall with a bang, the noise loud enough to make Lexi flinch and send water sloshing.

"Brodey!" She slammed the glass down and shook water off her hand. "A little warning would have helped."

How many times would he scare the daylights out of her tonight?

"Exactly," he said.

Grabbing napkins from the counter, she patted her hand dry. "So you meant to give me a bath in my living room?"

"Where's the glass?"

She rolled her eyes and wiped the floor. What a mess. "I put it down."

"That's the point. You put the glass down. If Williams heard an intruder in the laundry room, late at night, would he be carrying a glass?"

"I don't know. Maybe he was in the kitchen getting water."

"Maybe. But he'd still put the glass down. Think about it. Can't fight a guy with a glass in your hand. Unless he was gonna throw it at him. But let's say he didn't do that and he carried it into the laundry room with him."

"Okay."

"What does that indicate?"

Something told her this would take a while. Might as well eat while he did his detective thing. She sat again, grabbed her dish and swung back to him. "I have no idea."

"How about he didn't feel threatened? He wasn't surprised by whoever was in there."

"What if he knew the person?"

Brodey rolled one hand. "Right. And according to autopsy reports, the time of death was after eleven o'clock. Who would be coming to his house in the middle of the night? Think about it."

A lover. Or… Oh no.

"Come on, Lex, I know you have it."

"Okay, but if a family member—"

"Maybe his wife."

Narrowing her eyes, she waved a finger at him. "If a *family* member did it, why didn't the original detectives figure that out?"

Brodey returned to his seat, gave her a light, backhanded pat on her leg and dug into his food. Second time he'd done that patting thing. Affectionate man. Something to get used to, considering she'd never been overly affectionate in the physical sense. Growing up, her parents didn't subscribe to touchy-feely and the pig of a cheating ex-fiancé—God, she refused to even say his name—wasn't much into PDA. Unless, of course, it included his intern.

And his desk.

But now, sitting with Brodey, suddenly touchy-feely seemed…nice.

"We detectives have theories," he said. "Particularly the old-timers. Once they get a scent of something, tunnel vision can set in. They latch on to something and lose their open mind. I could see them liking the intruder-through-the-open-window theory and—*bam*—case solved."

Remind her never to get murdered, because the idea of detectives incorrectly latching on to a theory terrified her. Appetite destroyed, she tossed her fork into the bowl. "That's not comforting."

He shrugged. "It happens. No one does it to hurt a case. Usually."

This just kept getting better and better. She swiveled sideways and faced him. "What now?"

"That's easy. Now I pay a visit to his wife and any close friends and see who came over to the house a lot." He stood, dropped a quick kiss on her lips. "I gotta go. Thanks for dinner."

"You barely touched it."

"I know. Duty calls. I'll call you if I find anything."

Chapter Seven

First thing Monday morning, Lexi stood in the hallway outside the Williamses' master bedroom watching Nate rip up more dirty-snow carpet. This family loved beige. And not even a decent one at that.

But thankfully, dirty-beige carpeting was the only thing she needed to think about this morning. Considering she'd tossed and turned two nights straight obsessing over Brodey's kiss. She couldn't even blame her restlessness on lust. Hardly so. Calling his kiss chaste would be an overstatement. The ease with which that kiss was delivered, that casual peck, as if he kissed her that way every night and should be used to it, had thrown her. Thrown her enough that she'd kept her distance from him the day before by using work as an excuse. Not a complete lie, but not altogether the truth, either.

In her mind, men were lying pigs who couldn't be trusted. Getting used to anything with a man, falling into a casual routine and becoming too complacent, had been the catalyst to her not sensing her beloved spent his lunches *interfacing* with his intern.

"Whoops," Nate said.

Whoops what? Lexi hated *whoops*. Just as she stepped into the room, he pressed two fingers along the baseboard.

"Loose baseboard. I'll replace it."

With that, he tore off six inches of board and tossed it into the pile of scraps behind him.

"Now, that's weird," Lexi said. "Why would only that small piece be loose?"

She squatted to check the rest of the board between the closet and the bathroom. "Someone definitely cut this in half."

If the baseboard needed replacing, why not replace the entire section? Why just this small piece? In a house of this quality, she'd expect the owner to spring for the thirty dollars it would take to replace the entire board. Unless there was a reason. Couple that with someone being murdered in this house and her curiosity exploded. At this point, everything was questionable. She glanced at her winter-white slacks—*need to risk it*—and dropped to her stomach, laying her cheek against the carpet. If she soiled her clothes, she'd go home and change. Simple as that.

She peeked into the opening. Too dark. "Got a flashlight?"

Nate shined his penlight into the opening. Behind the cobwebs she spotted a small notebook similar to the little black books men used to joke about. Mystery solved. "There's something in there."

"What?"

"Looks like an address book."

She reached in, hesitated for half a second because somewhere down deep a flicker of warning hit her system. *Don't touch it.* But with the amount of cobwebs, who knew how long it had been there. It was probably nothing.

But she'd never know unless she looked. Shoving her hand farther in, she felt the gauzy slide of cobwebs close over her hand—ugh. Definitely washing up after this. She dragged the book from its hiding spot and brushed dust from the faux-leather cover.

Only a few pages had handwritten entries. Not someone's everyday calendar. Unless the person led a seriously boring life.

But, *hmm.* She flipped to December, the month of the murder, and thumbed through each page. On December 16, someone—presumably Jonathan Williams—wrote *CLEANER* across the top of the page along with a Chicago phone number. Had she just found evidence? If so, her fingerprints were now all over it.

Again the flutter of panic—the warning she'd ignored thirty seconds ago—came to life. What she probably—no *probably* about it—should have done was call Brodey.

Too late for that.

"What is it?" Nate asked.

"An appointment book."

"Hidden in the wall?" He peeked over her shoulder. "I bet he didn't want his wife to see it. Why else would it be in the wall?"

"They were separated?"

"Not for that long. He probably stuck it in there when they were still together."

Typical male response. "You don't think his wife would have noticed that loose baseboard?"

Nate shrugged. "You didn't and you look for stuff like that. Plus, how do we know there wasn't a chair or dresser in front of it?"

Men just had an answer for everything. She held up the open book. "What do you think *CLEANER* means? Housekeeper?"

"No idea. Call the number. I guarantee a woman will answer. I'm telling you, he hid this from his wife."

Okay, smart guy. For no other reason than to prove him wrong, she'd do it. She dug her cell phone from her jacket pocket. "Read me the number. I'll bet you lunch you're wrong."

Nate read off the number and Lexi punched the speaker button. Three rings later someone picked up. "Yeah?"

Male voice.

Distinctive. Rough. As if nails had scraped his vocal cords, leaving them damaged and raw.

I know that voice.

"Who is this?" the man said.

Definitely him. The creep who'd talked to her on the sidewalk yesterday. The creep she'd drawn the sketch of. The creep Brodey couldn't find.

Panic, swift and obliterating, shot straight up Lexi's neck. *Hang up, hang up, hang up.* She poked at the screen, pounding it with her index finger until the call disconnected.

"A man," Nate said. "Now, *that's* interesting. I guess I owe you lunch."

She glanced up at Nate and sickness poured into her stomach, flip-flopping her morning coffee.

Nate cocked his head. Studied her for a second. "You okay? You look a little sick."

I am sick. And she needed to get out of this house before The Creep realized it was her calling his number and came looking for her. "I'm fine. I…uh…need to make calls. Will you take care of this?"

"Sure. I'll let you know when we're wrapped up here."

She charged down the steps, teetering on her high heels and praying she didn't land on her face along the way. At the moment, she wasn't sure what would be worse, the face-plant or Brodey's reaction to her calling that number. Either way, it would be trouble.

At the base of the stairs she stopped, stared at the front door and gasped. What if that creep was out there somewhere? Watching her. Brodey had warned he could be keeping an eye on the place. And she'd be walking to her car alone.

Can't do it.

She'd have to stay here—inside with Nate upstairs. At least she wasn't alone.

And when Brodey heard this news, he'd go crazy. The lecture he'd level on her would turn her to stone. Her own fault for not thinking through her actions, for not calling him when she saw that notebook and for not listening to her instincts when they told her not to touch it.

The latch on the front door thunked. *Him.* But how would he know it was she who had called?

"Nate!"

She backed up a step, her heel catching on the stair as she kept her gaze glued to the bottom of the front door when it opened. A man's boot hit the threshold. She brought her gaze up along the jean-clad leg to the worn leather jacket—she knew that jacket—and the arm tucked in a sling under it. Her breath caught.

"Brodey?"

He popped his head in. "Hi."

Gushing blood pounded at her temples and she pressed her palms against her head. *I'm not alone.* Slowly, focusing on Brodey, she inhaled, held it a second and exhaled until the pounding eased.

"What's up?" Nate called from the landing above.

She tilted her head up. "Nothing. False alarm."

"You are wigging out on me today."

Nate disappeared and she turned back to Brodey. "I'm so happy to see you right now."

He grinned. "I like that greeting. But you look like hell."

She rushed down the stairs, careful not to move too fast and tumble down. A trip to the hospital would be the capper. "You're going to be really upset with me and I'm sorry. I didn't... Ugh."

"Oh, boy. What'd you do?"

She held the appointment book in her hand, contemplated the lecture she'd get and shoved it at him.

Slowly, he shifted his gaze to her hand. "What's this?"

"I found it. Upstairs. Behind a piece of loose baseboard. I touched it. I'm sorry."

He puckered, but didn't take the book. Instead, he slid his free hand into the messenger bag slung over his shoulder and retrieved a pair of latex gloves.

The silence alone, from a man who took great pride in offering his opinions, made her stomach bunch. "Um, there's an entry on December 16."

"Uh-huh."

"With a phone number."

He snapped on the gloves and went back to the book, his fingers riffling through the pages.

Time to fess up. Now or never. "I called the number."

"Somehow," he said, his voice low and calm, "I knew you'd say that."

She hated that voice. From him she wanted sarcasm and lecturing—maybe even yelling. This calm? It terrified her. "I'm sorry. I got carried away. Nate and I were debating why the book was hidden and he figured Jonathan hid it from his wife because it had phone numbers for women in it."

"Okay, well, that's a leap."

"I thought so, too, and to prove my point, dialed the number. I didn't think it through."

"An issue, for sure. After the guy from yesterday, anything you find in this house could be evidence."

The lecturing voice again. Good. That she could deal with. "I got caught up."

And if he thought he was irritated by her handling the book, wait'll he heard who answered.

He held up a gloved hand. "Let's argue about it later. You said you called the number."

"Yes."

"Did a woman answer?"

"No. A man. And I recognized the voice."

SHE RECOGNIZED THE VOICE. Of all the things Brodey thought she might say, that one knocked him sideways. Whether or not she actually recognized the voice or simply thought she recognized the voice had yet to be determined. At times, witnesses were sure what they saw.

Until they weren't.

Lexi stood on the first step, eye to eye with him, her greenish-brown eyes lacking that Lexi spunk. Nope. What he saw here was stone-cold fear. "You're fine. Okay? Don't panic. Who do you think it was?"

"I don't think—I know. It was that creepy guy from yesterday."

Damn it. Forget not panicking because it was definitely time to panic. He wouldn't tell her that, though. He nudged her to a sitting position on the step and settled in next to her. "How do you know?"

"He has a distinctive voice. Really raw."

"Uh-huh."

"It was him. I know it was."

Brodey opened the book to December 16, where *CLEANER* had been written across the top. That could mean anything. Cleaning lady, a trip to the dry cleaner's, carpet cleaning.

An assassin.

But if it was the number for an assassin and Williams wanted to hire him—for what reason Brodey didn't know—why would Williams be the one dead? He needed to find this guy. Fast.

Not only did Brodey want the 411 on him, the guy now had Lexi's cell number. Brodey ran his fingers over his forehead and squeezed. With that cell number, any halfway resourceful person, particularly a criminal with connections, could easily find her address. Assuming she'd used her phone and not Nate's to place that call.

He let out a long breath. "You called on your cell? Or Nate's?"

"Mine."

"Of course you did."

"Sorry."

"You're making me crazy." He waved the

address book. "You've got to stop and think about what you're doing."

"I know."

Did she? He wasn't sure because she continued to do things that put her in danger. "It doesn't feel like you do. You need to consider ramifications. Now, whoever this guy is, if he tried, he'd figure out where you live."

She closed her eyes. "I shouldn't have called that number. Part of me knew it and then I blew that part off. I'm so sorry."

"Hey, it's done now. We'll deal with it. Anything in this house could be evidence, though. Treat it as such. Don't touch it until you call me. Got it?"

She nodded. "Got it."

"Good. I'll run the phone number and see what we find."

"Shouldn't we give this information to the police?"

"Maybe. We don't know what we have yet. The guy on the other end of that call could have been a poker buddy of our victim."

She considered that, then held her hands out. "You're not even supposed to be working on this case. How will you trace that number?"

Carefully, that was how. He boosted off the step, grabbed his messenger bag with his laptop and headed for the kitchen. "The wonders of the internet. Amazing what a credit card and online research will get you. Even if I strike out on who the number belongs to, I should be able to find out if it's a cell number. Guessing it is. If so, let's hope it's a carrier I have a contact with."

"And then?"

"And then I get a name, run him through the system and see if our boy here has a rap sheet. If he's ever been accused of murder, I'd say we have a suspect."

In the kitchen, Brodey swung his messenger bag onto the island, used his free hand to drag his laptop out and booted it up. The night before, with his sister AWOL on another case and Brodey unable to sleep after striking out on contacting Mrs. Williams regarding her husband's friends, he'd downloaded and scanned all the reports he'd obtained on this case. If his hard copies suddenly went missing, he now had a backup. Yeah, he always planned for the worst. Couldn't help it.

Thanks to the hot spot from his phone, he clicked on the icon for his browser. Lexi stood next to him, not too close, but close enough that she once again upset the energy around him. From the second he'd put eyes on her, she upset his energy.

Massively.

"Read me the number again."

He entered the digits into the search engine, and a list of options for obtaining information on phone numbers popped up. He didn't recognize any of the sites. Probably bogus. The truly easy thing to do right here would be to call one of his buddies at the station and have him run the number, but seeing as he shouldn't be working on this, he couldn't risk anyone in a jackpot with him.

But his sister had gotten him into this in the first place. Blame it on her.

"Time-out." He grabbed his phone off the counter and scrolled to Jenna's number. "My sister can get us this info."

Voice mail. He left her the phone number, told her what he needed, hung up and sent her a text. "Give her ten minutes. Guaranteed."

"That fast?"

"She's an animal."

Six minutes later, his phone rang. Jenna. "Called it." He hit the button. "Hey. Whatcha got?"

As usual, she dispatched with the pleasantries. "That number belongs to one Ed Long. He lives on the West Side. Who is he?"

"Don't know. Lexi found an appointment book at Williamses' house. The number was written in on December 16."

"Stop it! That's the day he died."

"Sure is. I'm gonna run this guy down, see if he's in the system."

"I thought you were worried about getting caught."

"I am. Which is why I'm gonna ask Dad to call in a favor or two. Text me Long's address. While Dad's doing his thing, Lexi and I will pay a visit and see if he's the guy in her sketch."

As MUCH AS she wanted an assistant, Lexi didn't think chasing down a suspected murderer would get it for her. After all, what good would the assistant do her if she were dead? "We're going to his *house*?"

"Bet your life," Brodey said. "I want to know if he's the guy you saw. And if the address is valid." He went back to his laptop. "Let's do an internet search on him."

"You're *searching for* him?"

"Is there a reason you keep repeating my statements?"

"Uh, shock maybe?"

He smiled and pounded the enter key. "You're cute."

"Better cute than dead, handsome. Know what I mean?"

"This is not a big deal. You'll stay in the car." He turned away from the computer, leaned one hip against the island and ran the roughened tips of his fingers along her jawline, a slow, tender sensation that made the girl who never much liked PDA want to reconsider her stance.

"Brodey—"

"I wouldn't let anything happen to you. You know that, don't you?"

Yes. She did. Absolutely. He had that protective—not to mention stubborn—streak in him. Her own modern-day Hercules this one. Plus, if he didn't stop stroking her jaw… "I know that. It makes me nervous is all. Like he knows me, but I don't know him."

"Which is why we're tracking him." He dropped his hand, waggled his eyebrows and went back to his laptop. "I always do a search on a suspect. You find all kinds of stuff on the internet. Even if it isn't rocket science, why not use every tool available? Whoa. Lots of Ed Longs. Okay. Let's narrow this down." He went back to the search bar and typed in *Ed Long Chicago Illinois* with his free hand. "Let's see what we get now."

"We could go back to you rubbing my face. That was a whole lot nicer than the thought of coming face-to-face with Creep Man."

Again, he turned to her, slid one hand under her blazer, and suddenly she wanted that sling gone, wanted both of his hands on her as he patted her hip. "I promise you, this'll be okay.

For all we know, he probably teaches kindergarten. Don't worry about it until there's something to worry about."

She stepped a tiny bit closer, her body craving the heat and security that came with Brodey Hayward. Security. Something she'd never wanted or needed from a man. At this moment the independent career girl in her, the one who'd marched out of her loser fiancé's office swearing she'd never allow herself to need a man, the one who constantly reminded her that men were dishonest, rutting animals, didn't have much to say. Now the career girl went on hiatus? She squeezed her eyes closed. *So confused.*

"Lex?"

Subject change. That was what they needed right now. And given this whole mess, she had plenty of choices. "I could have destroyed evidence with that damned book."

"We'll work around it. The book might not even be his. Maybe it's the previous owner's."

She gave him a baleful look. "Nice try."

Then something changed. His smile—that flashing quickness that, when unleashed, could do a girl in—faded, and she locked her jaw. Where he focused so intently, his gaze on hers, his mouth soft, no tightness, could do a girl in worse than the smile. *I'm a mess.* She forced herself to stay quiet. With that look, who knew what went on in his brain? In addition to being rutting animals, men had tendencies to say the exact opposite of what a woman wanted to hear. Maybe he'd lecture her again on being more careful and less spontaneous. Maybe he wouldn't. All she knew was, on a purely physical level, she wanted whatever Brodey Hayward had in mind.

He inched closer, tipped his head sideways. "I hope you're aware that I'm extremely attracted to you."

"In fact, I wasn't. Not really. Well, it sort of felt like—"

"Stop."

"What?"

"Talking. We don't need to analyze. A yes-or-no answer would have done it."

"Yes. Now I'm aware. For sure."

He grinned. "Close enough. Thank you."

"You're welcome."

"So, Lexi."

"So, Brodey."

"If I were to ask you to dinner, what would you say?"

"I'd say maybe. After I get this project done."

"Ouch."

She stepped closer, the collar of his jacket barely two inches from her lips and the clean scent of his soap lingering on him. She inhaled, loving the closeness. If she looked up, she'd be useless. All her nights spent alone paraded in her brain, reminding her how much of a life she didn't have. "Please don't be offended. My life is a nightmare. I'm interviewing assistants, which I won't be able to afford unless I get this house sold. I'm averaging four hours of sleep a night because I'm building a business and refuse to turn clients away. A couple of more big clients and I'm on my way. That's what I want. To be self-sufficient. To have a safety net."

No rutting animals.

"I get that. But you have to eat."

"I eat while I'm working."

He went back to his laptop. "No problem. Tonight, I'll call you and find out where you're working and I'll bring you dinner. I like that idea."

"Brodey—"

"Yes or no, Lex. That's all this requires."

Rutting animal or not, that hand on her hip, combined with the chin stroking from a minute ago, did amazing things to her libido.

"Come on, Lexi, live a little." He leaned in, got right next to her ear. "I promise I'll behave."

That tore it. If they didn't get back to the task at hand, she might do something really stupid and tilt her head sideways, just that small hint that—yes indeed—she would like to revisit kissing him. Yes indeed. "Yes. To…uh…dinner."

Smooth, Lexi.

He backed away. "Excellent. Now, let's get back to work before I convince you to let me do things to you on this island."

And just that fast, he went back to his laptop. "Yow. Check. It. Out. Hello, Ed Long."

"You found him. Is there a photo?"

He clicked on a link that led to a local newspaper article from six years ago. "No photo. If this is our Ed Long, he was arrested on robbery charges." He whistled. "Did three years."

"Oh my."

"Don't panic. He's not a murderer. Nothing here indicates violence. Money motivates him, not blood."

Brodey dug a notepad from his messenger bag and, sling and all, jotted notes. "Let's check the address we have. If it's still good and you recognize him, I'll go see his lawyer. The lawyer won't tell me much, but it never hurts."

Did she need an assistant enough to risk visiting a potential murderer?

No.

Not unless she intended to have a life again. If she went and was able to identify Ed Long, it might move this investigation along. In turn, allowing her to complete the renovations and get the house sold.

Debating the assistant-versus-no-assistant dilemma, she tilted her head one way, then the other. Sleep. That was what she needed. Sleep would happen when she hired an assistant.

"Okay," she said.

"Good. Let's do this." He squeezed her arm. "This'll be good. Trust me. I'll take care of it."

She believed that. She believed when Brodey Hayward put his mind to something, nothing stopped him. Why she felt that way, she wasn't quite sure, but the way he entered a room, that commanding presence, his ability to take charge of a situation—no matter what that situation— she imagined he always took care of it.

"I know you will. I don't know how I know, but I do. And I like that. It doesn't happen very often."

"You? Really? I thought you were the trusting one."

"I am, but this is different. I trust people until I *don't* trust them. I'm not stupid and I won't hand a stranger my life's savings. But you? I might give you my life's savings, and I'm not sure I'm happy about it."

In truth, it terrified her.

Above her, something crashed. She glanced

up at the ceiling, hoping a sink didn't plummet through.

"It's fine!" Nate yelled from upstairs.

"Thank you!" She went back to Brodey. "All I need is him putting a hole in the ceiling."

"Can I ask you something?"

"Sure."

"How old are you?"

"Twenty-nine."

He pulled a face. "Wow."

"What does 'wow' mean?"

After closing the laptop, he slid it into his messenger bag. "It's good. You're twenty-nine and managing contractors who've probably been in this business longer than that, if I'm any good at guessing Nate's age. You're fearless. I don't know many women like you. Well, except my sister, but she's twisted that way. She grew up surrounded by cops. That fearlessness scares the hell out of me, but it's impressive. You're impressive. Makes me wonder why you don't like trusting me. Then again, maybe that's why you haven't let a man snag you."

Rutting animals. "I almost did. We were engaged. Last year."

"Uh-oh."

"One day I walked past a jewelry store downtown and saw a wedding ring that I loved. I was a few blocks from my so-called beloved's office so I swung by there to tell him about my find." She smiled a little, let that feeling of happiness come back to her. Occasionally, she liked to think about those moments, the joy and excitement as she raced the three blocks to tell him the great news. "I was so happy. Probably the happiest I'd ever been."

"What'd he say?"

The memory, as it always did, faded to that second when her world broke apart. "I never got a chance to tell him. I opened the door to his office and found him on top of his twenty-year-old intern."

"Come on! That is *harsh*."

"And incredibly cliché, don't you think?"

"Oh, man."

"I was so humiliated." She flapped her arms. "I mean, how does that happen? He's the one doing a college student—never mind his employee—on his desk, and I'm humiliated?"

Again, he reached up, ran one of his big, giant and incredibly warm hands down the side of her head. "What'd you do?"

She shrugged. "I walked out. Left the door open so everyone could see, and I walked out. I was dead inside, but I wasn't about to let his entire office see me come apart. I saved that for when I got home. Had a good cry over it, then I got mad. I packed every bit of his stuff up and told him the box would be on my door-step at eight o'clock. Then I deleted him from my contacts."

Brodey laughed. "Damn, I love that. He deserved it."

"You know it. I'll forgive, but I don't forget. He hurt me and no matter how many times he begged, I didn't see myself ever having faith in him again."

"And you think that was unfair? After he betrayed you?"

She shrugged. "I don't know."

"He was messing around. You think he wouldn't have done that after the wedding? No. He got what he deserved. If he was smart, he learned from it. Seriously, I don't get guys like that. I mean, I'm no saint, I like sex as much as the next guy, but if you're gonna make that commitment, stick to it. If you wanna be off-leash, then don't make the commitment. What's the big deal?"

"Exactly!"

"Guys are stupid sometimes. What can I say?"

Lexi laughed. "You know, Brodey Hayward, you might be part woman underneath all this machismo."

His face distorted, his lips peeling back into a look that indicated she might be next in line for the electric chair. "What does that mean?"

"You're just…reasonable. You get it. A lot of men don't. And I also think I may wind up sleeping with you."

"Uh, pardon me," Nate said.

She spun back, heat not just creeping but sizzling up her neck. Nate was not blind, nor was he stupid, but being a good man, seeing Lexi's embarrassment, he turned his attention to the molding above the doorway, running his hand over it. "We may need to replace this."

Sure they did.

The inferno raging in Lexi's cheeks cooled. She just might get out of this disaster. "Everything okay?"

Behind her, Brodey brushed his hand along her lower back, distracting her, reminding her that for the past year, the majority of her life had been spent alone, without simple touches of affection. Even for a woman who disliked PDA, she craved the basic comfort of human touch.

"Yeah," Nate said. "I…uh…need to run and check on another job site. It'll take about an hour. Will you be okay here?"

Earlier, she'd told him about her experience with the supposed neighbor who wasn't a neighbor and, not surprisingly, he'd agreed with Brodey about her not being alone in the house.

"She's good," Brodey said.

Oh. She was, was she? One soul-baring

conversation and suddenly he was in charge? She shot him a look.

"I'm not bossing you around. We just said you'd go with me to check this guy out. See if he matched the sketch. That's all."

She hesitated, ticked back the conversation. "You're right. I'm sorry."

"So, we're squared away here?" Nate asked.

"Yes, thank you. Apparently I'm going on a suspect hunt."

BRODEY DROVE PAST the broken-down duplex that matched the address Jenna had given him for Ed Long. The rental sign stuck into the front lawn, if that small patch of dirt mixed with splotches of dormant grass could be considered a lawn, didn't look promising. Could be for the adjoining unit.

Otherwise, Ed Long was in the wind.

In the passenger seat, Lexi fiddled with her phone—probably checking emails. Or ignoring him after she'd announced that maybe she'd give him a shot in the sack. An announcement he couldn't drop-kick from his mind. Yep, when he got her alone again, he'd make up for lost time. For now, she could ignore him all she wanted.

"Hey," she said, "what are you smiling about?"

"You, actually."

"Me?"

"Yep. Thinking about getting you alone again makes me a happy boy."

He'd heard silence before, brutal silence that made him twitch, but this went beyond that. Beautiful Lexi Vanderbilt sat beside him, her eyes wide and focused and her breaths coming in short, uneven bursts. Total panic attack. He patted her leg. "Relax."

"I…don't have a lot of free time. I can't drop everything. And thinking about squeezing… uh… Wow…bad word choice." She winced. "I don't have room for a lot in my insane life. And I don't want you mad at me."

"Who says I'll be mad at you? We had a conversation. It doesn't equal a lifetime commitment."

"You're okay with that?"

"I'm thirty-two years old and have never come close to considering marriage. I'd say, yeah, I'm okay with that." Her head snapped back—whoops—a little sensitivity might have been in order there. *Way to go, Brodey.* "That sounded bad. Probably should have worded it differently."

"I'd rather have the truth. I'm a lunatic about it. No secrets or lies. It's vital to me, so I appreciate you being so up-front. You're looking for fun. I get it."

Was he? A few months ago, definitely. After

grueling twelve-hour days, a hot woman, a warm bed and no attachments worked fine. Just fine. Now, being on disability, bored out of his skull in his empty apartment, drove him crazy enough to realize the definite lack of a relationship wasn't so great.

And then his mother cracked that joke about him needing to find a wife so he'd stop coming over and disrupting her schedule. *Thanks, Mom.*

Even his mother had dumped him.

Half a block from the busted-up duplex, he snagged a parking spot. "Okay," he said. "Wait here. I'm gonna knock on the door. See if he answers."

"Wait. What if he recognizes you? If he's been watching the Williamses' place, he'll have seen you coming and going."

Before getting into the car, he'd ditched his sling and now slowly reached into the backseat. He grabbed a skullcap, shoved it on his head along with his sunglasses. Instant disguise. "If he's seen me, he's never gotten close enough to recognize me with the hat and glasses. Sit tight. Lock the doors."

He slid his ASP expandable baton from under the seat, shoved it into his back pocket and started the trek. Hunched against the wind, he shoved his hands into his pockets to retain any heat possible. Damned frigid weather. To distract himself, he counted down the addresses. Next unit on the left was Long's, and not for the first time Brodey wished he'd had his badge and sidearm. At least he had the ASP. No self-respecting cop walked into a situation like this without a weapon. If necessary, he could snap a bone with that baton.

If necessary.

He opened the aluminum screen door and winced at the squeak. Catching the door with his foot, he wedged between it and hammered on the inside door.

Nothing.

In another few seconds, he'd bang on it again. Harder. The door to the adjoining unit opened, revealing a more-than-middle-aged guy in a stained white T-shirt and flannel pants. His thinning gray hair stuck up on one side and grid lines dented his left cheek. *Late sleeper.* Considering it was almost lunchtime.

"You here about the rental?" he croaked. "Give me a second. I'll get the key."

Now, on a normal visit like this, Brodey would badge the guy and identify himself. Not today. This visit, he'd be a lowlife looking for another lowlife.

"Nah." He gestured to the door in front of him. "Lookin' for Ed. You seen him?"

The man's face pinched. "That no-good bum? He burned me on a month's rent. Haven't seen the SOB."

Well, damn. "He skipped?"

"Three weeks ago yesterday. Took his stuff and went. Left the trash, though. I had to clean that stinking mess. If you find him, tell him I'm looking for him. And I'm keeping his security deposit."

Brodey glanced at the door leading to Ed Long's now-vacant apartment and considered asking for a peek.

The landlord jerked his thumb toward Long's former living unit. "Why're you lookin' for him? I don't want no trouble here."

Brodey reached into his jacket pocket and unfolded the copy of the sketch Lexi had done, let the landlord have a look. "We go back a ways. My sister saw him a week or so ago. She's an artsy type and drew this sketch of him. I didn't recognize him with longer hair." He snatched the sketch back and shoved it into his pocket again. "Figured I'd track him down and see what he was up to."

"Your sister is pretty good. He had that long hair the whole time he lived here. Two years he made on-time rent payments. Then he skipped on me."

"Yeah, well, sorry 'bout that. I'll rip him one when I see him."

The landlord shivered against the frigid air. "Yeah. Thanks."

Brodey made his way back to Lexi and his Jeep SUV. As he approached, the door locks clunked. Lexi must have hit the button. He hopped back into the vehicle, plucked the skull cap off and tossed it over his shoulder. "No dice."

She cocked her head, studying him for a second before lifting her hand—*what's she doing?*—and mashing down one side of his hair. He would have liked to say something about that being nice or whatever, but she'd likely freak on him, so he'd keep those thoughts to himself. Wouldn't stop him from fantasizing about other things she could be doing with those hands.

She finished fiddling with his hair and sat back again, apparently unaffected. She may have been unmoved, but not his nervous system. Nope. That sucker couldn't have been more alert. He shook it off. "Thanks. For fixing my hair."

"Sure. It looked cute, but I didn't think you'd want to be walking around like that. You have great hair, by the way. It's wavy, but not curly."

"Yeah. Used to make me nuts. Then I gave up trying to control it. Wherever it lands, it lands."

"With the right cut, it doesn't matter."

"I've learned. And believe me, I take a ton of garbage from my brother because the only person I've found who can deal with it works in a swanky salon in the Loop. Sixty dollars to cut my damned hair. On my salary. My brother pays fifteen."

"Yes, but your brother's hair probably doesn't look—or act—like yours."

"My point exactly!"

Irritated over his trip to Long's being a bust—not to mention thinking about that damned sixty dollars—he slid the car into gear and hit the gas.

"I guess Mr. Long wasn't home? Or is the rental sign for his place?"

"He skipped three weeks ago. Landlord can't find him. And, just so you know—" Brodey cleared his throat, readying for his croaking impression of the landlord "—he's keeping the security deposit that no-good bum left."

Lexi laughed. "Did you show him the sketch? Is it him?"

At the traffic light, Brodey glanced at her, grinning like an idiot because he'd made her laugh. "Yeah. It's him."

As expected, her laughter died. Boom. Gone.

"Lex, it's okay. It's part of the process. We'll find him. Next stop is his lawyer. Somehow, their lawyers always know where to find these guys."

Chapter Eight

Lexi's voice mail was full.

At least that was what the email from Nate, delivered via her phone, told her. Full. How many voice mails could that be? Scratch that. She didn't want to know. It would only stress her out. Spending the morning running around with Brodey, as easy as he was on the eyes, didn't do her business a bit of good.

He parked in a small lot adjacent to the three-story brick office building on the Far West Side of Chicago. "This is it. The lawyer is on the first floor. You coming in?"

Returning calls should have been her priority. But how many times did a girl get to ride shotgun with a hot detective about to question someone? Forget the calls. "Yes. I'm going in. I'm curious. Do you have the sketch? I have extra copies in my briefcase."

"Grab one. Mine is crumpled from being in my pocket." He grinned. "We don't want to appear unprofessional after you've coiffed my hair."

Seriously, she could jump him. "Heavens no."

An icy parking lot and sidewalk made for a life-threatening expedition, and Lexi decided a good detective shouldn't wear heels while on an assignment. They'd managed to enter the office, a first-floor unit badly in need of updating from its '90s decor, and a woman in her sixties, also in need of updating, greeted them.

Brodey plastered on another jump-worthy smile and Lexi's toes curled.

"Hello," he said. "Is Henry available?"

The woman eyed him, but shifted forward slightly, her body clearly submitting to the pressure of Brodey in full-on charm mode. "Did you have an appointment?"

An appointment. Lexi glanced at the three metal-framed and extremely empty chairs lining the outside wall. The faux leather had enough dirt to seal a bleeding wound. She would, without question, remain standing.

The good detective turned the wattage up on his smile and leaned in, meeting his new love slave halfway. "Do we need one?"

Wicked, wicked boy.

"Generally," the receptionist said. "But let me see if he's available. Who should I say is calling?"

"Brodey Hayward. Chicago PD Homicide."

All along he'd been insisting on keeping his identity quiet, and suddenly he was practically flashing a badge.

The receptionist hung up. "He'll see you now, Detective." The woman pointed to the door behind her. "Right through that door."

"Terrific. Thank you."

"Of course."

And, hey, Grandma just checked out *Brodey's* rear. Backsides were popular with these two. Boundaries, people. *Boundaries.*

Lexi shook her head as they stepped into the cramped office of Henry Blade, Esq. Surprisingly young, maybe mid-thirties, considering the man's office hadn't been renovated in twenty years, Henry stood to greet them. "Detective, nice to meet you. I'm Henry."

The two men shook hands and Henry turned to Lexi, hitting her with his own winning smile. His couldn't compete with Brodey's, but he was no slouch, either. "Hello," he said.

Lexi extended her hand. "Hello. I'm Alexis Vanderbilt."

"Are you a detective, also?"

"No." She couldn't help herself. "I'm an interior designer."

One your office needs.

"Oh," he said.

If he wondered why a homicide detective and an interior designer were in his office, he didn't show it. In his line of work, he probably met all kinds. She certainly did.

"Have a seat. What can I help you folks with?"

Lexi glanced at the two guest chairs, found the upholstered cushions infinitely cleaner than the ones in the waiting room and sat.

Brodey did the same, his big shoulders filling the chair, his gaze focused with such intense confidence that it would terrify mere mortals. God, this man. So hot in a truly annoying way that left Lexi ready to slap him *and* snuggle up all at the same time.

"We're looking for one of your clients," he said.

"I see. Obviously, I can't share any information about cases with you."

"I realize that. We're not interested in your cases. All we want is to locate Ed Long."

"Ed Long?"

"Yes, sir."

Henry propped one elbow on the armrest. "Hell, I haven't seen him in two years."

Two years. She was no detective, but with Jonathan Williams being dead for that long, the timing fit.

"Is he in trouble again?"

Brodey shrugged. "Not sure yet. He approached

Ms. Vanderbilt at one of her job sites and there've been some thefts in the area."

A lie. But there could have been thefts. Who knew? Henry glanced at her, but didn't ask why a witness would be tagging along on this little jaunt. Whatever his concerns, he went back to Brodey. "And you think Ed did it?"

"I didn't say that. We'd like to talk to him about why he was in the area."

"What area was this?"

"Cartright," Brodey said.

A few seconds passed with Henry eyeballing Brodey and Brodey eyeballing right back.

Eventually, Henry lost the battle. "I, uh, once knew someone who lived in Cartright. Our kids went to preschool together."

"Let me guess. Jonathan Williams?"

Henry lurched back, his poker face disintegrating. "How'd you know that?"

Now, this was fascinating.

"Ms. Vanderbilt is doing work on Mr. Williams's home. His widow is trying to sell it."

Henry finally looked over at her. "And Ed was there?"

She pulled the sketch from her briefcase and set it on the desk. "A man pretending to be a neighbor stopped me in front of the house and asked questions. I drew this sketch of him."

"You recognize him?" Brodey asked.

After studying the sketch for a few seconds, Henry put his poker face back together. "Looks like him. He claimed he was a neighbor?"

"Yes, sir."

Back in lawyer mode, Henry sat back again. "I'm sorry. I can't help you. Not only would I be sanctioned by the bar, as I said, I haven't seen him in years."

"I understand." Brodey pushed out of his chair and extended his hand. "Thanks for your time."

"Of course."

That was it? All the way over here for that? Lexi opened her mouth, but Brodey had already stridden to the door and opened it. So confusing, this detective work. And she'd blown off clients for this. Sighing, she followed him to the outer office, where the love slave looked up from her paperwork and smiled. "You have a great day, now."

"Thanks," Brodey said. "You, too."

When they hit the sidewalk, Brodey latched on to Lexi's elbow, hanging on to her so she didn't slide across the ice. "They should salt this," he said. "Someone could get hurt."

On that, they agreed. "Why'd you give up so fast?"

"Give up? I'm just getting started. He's a lawyer clamming up. But he told us he knew Williams. That's damned intriguing." He unlocked the Jeep SUV and pulled her door open. "With him knowing Williams *and* Ed Long, we now have a connection. All we have to do is figure out where and when Ed made that connection."

"Okay. How do we do that?"

"We see if he ever visited the Williamses' home."

"Which means asking Brenda."

"Yep."

Please. He couldn't honestly believe Brenda Williams, a woman who loved her children more than life, would be involved in their father's murder? "You're not thinking she's a suspect?"

"I'm not thinking anything. Just chasing down a lead."

BRODEY PARKED HIMSELF on Brenda Williams's sofa and scooted to the edge of the cushion, his back straighter than a solid-steel pipe, his face completely neutral. Alert, attentive and non-threatening. He'd assumed this position many times when speaking with a witness. Or in really rotten situations, a devastated family member. In this case, he wasn't sure what the hell Brenda was.

Having a solid alibi, she'd been cleared early on, but how hard had the detectives looked at her on a conspiracy charge? With the mess her husband left—the lying, the millions he stole, the *humiliation*—it all added up to motive. Motive to collect life insurance by having her husband whacked.

Bam.

Beside him, Lexi leaned into the arm of the sofa. She'd been quiet since they'd left the lawyer's office, and it might have been the longest three hours of his life waiting for Brenda to get home. He hadn't wanted to leave Lexi alone and tagged along on her appointments to make sure she at least made it to and from her meetings without incident.

Chatter came from the kitchen, where the kids argued over a notebook. A minute later, the racket died down and Brenda entered the room, closing the French doors behind her. "Sorry. I wanted to get the kids squared away. It's always crazy around here right when they get home."

She dropped into the cushy chair across from Brodey, glanced at him and then to a miserable Lexi, who'd lost her game face somewhere. Either that or she stunk at masking her feelings.

"Is everything all right?"

He nodded. "Yes, ma'am. I wanted to show you a sketch. See if you recognize the man."

"Of course."

He slid the sketch from the folder he'd set on the coffee table and handed it to Brenda. "Take your time."

Before looking down, she met Brodey's gaze and held it. "Is he a suspect?"

"I'm not sure."

"Who is he?"

Unwilling to speculate on what Ed Long's involvement in her husband's death might have been, Brodey gestured to the photo. "Do you recognize him?"

The not-so-subtle hint that he wouldn't pony up intel worked and Brenda peered down at the photo. She tilted her head one way, then the other, her expression blank. Total gamer. Lexi could take a lesson from Brenda Williams on hiding her feelings.

She slid the paper away. "I don't think so. At least he's not someone I interacted with."

"Could he be a friend of your husband's?"

"Maybe. I didn't know all of Jonathan's associates."

"Mrs. Williams, I know you're trying to keep the children out of this. I get it. Believe me."

"But?"

Smart lady. "But after you and your husband split up, the children spent time alone with him at his house. They may have seen people coming and going."

"You want me to ask the children to look at the sketch."

Statement. Not a question. "Yes, ma'am. I apologize, but they may have seen him."

And if they saw him in the house, Brodey's theory on Williams possibly knowing his attacker—assuming Ed Long was that attacker— might be more than a theory. Which would cancel out his *other* theory that Brenda hired an assassin.

She sat back, her torso rolling forward as her body closed in on itself. Sometimes this job sucked the life right out of him. Sometimes? He'd just asked a mother, a woman he half suspected of murder, to possibly expose her children to emotional trauma and he had no problem justifying it. He glanced at Lexi, who twisted her lips in a noncommittal "sorry, dude, can't help you" look. Terrific.

But then she sat forward, resting her elbows on her knees, loosely clasping her hands together. "I'm not a mother. I cannot imagine what this feels like for you, and I'm sorry he has to ask this, but I've spent time with Brodey. He's not reckless and he wouldn't put your children through this if he didn't have to. If there was another way, he'd do it. I'm sure of that."

Nice. Finally in sync on something. And the bonus was she'd given him a compliment.

Brenda flicked a glance at him, then went back to Lexi. "Thank you for that."

"Of course."

She stood. "I'll bring them in together. They'll each take a turn looking at the sketch and then I'll have them leave again."

"If you want," Lexi said, "we can tell them I drew the sketch. It might be more interesting to them if they know that."

That stopped Brenda. "You drew it?"

"Yes. I saw him outside the house yesterday."

Cripes. What was she doing? Until they knew, without question, Ed Long's role here, there'd be no sharing of information. If Brenda knew him, she'd call and warn him the second they left. Brodey reached over, squeezed Lexi's arm to shut her the hell up. "Let's bring the kids in."

Sharp woman that she was, Brenda shot a look between them, knowing full well she didn't have the whole story.

"I'll be right back."

Brodey spun to Lexi, stretching closer so he wouldn't be overheard. Her long hair tickled his nose, made him want to bury his face in her neck, and what an inappropriate thought that was right now. "The less she knows the better. If she'd recognized him, that'd be one thing. She didn't. All we know is this guy was in the neighborhood. He could be casing homes and have nothing to do with this murder."

"I'm sorry."

"It's all right. Let's play it close to the vest until we figure out what his involvement is."

Children following behind, Brenda came through the doors again. She set her hand on the boy's head. "This is Sam. This is Patrice and our little squirt there is Meghan."

"Mama, I'm not a squirt."

"I know, baby. I just like calling you that. It makes me smile."

"Hey, guys." Brodey stayed in his spot on the sofa, eye level with the kids. No sense freaking them out by hovering. "So, here's what we're gonna do. Miss Lexi here is a pretty good artist." He motioned them to the coffee table. "In fact, she drew this picture."

"Cool!" Sam said.

"It is cool. How about you guys take a look at the picture and see if you recognize the person. Would that be okay?"

Sam shrugged. Meghan, all missing front teeth and pigtails, bobbed her head hard enough that the thing should have flown off. Patrice wandered closer, totally noncommittal, and Brodey's brain snapped.

What the snap meant, he'd find out soon enough, but generally that intensely visceral reaction meant someone knew something and in this bunch, eight-year-old Patrice might be the one.

Sam and Meghan flanked her while Brenda stood back, her shoulders dipped, body once again folding in. She glanced up, made solid eye contact and slowly pushed her shoulders back. For a woman in her thirties, she'd had her share of life's brutality. All Brodey needed to know was if she'd taken it upon herself to battle that brutality by killing her husband.

"I don't know him," Patrice said.

So much for instincts.

Meghan swung her head back and forth. "Me, neither."

Sam stayed silent. Interesting.

"Sam?" his mom said.

The kid shrugged. "I'm not sure."

Not. Sure. Brodey forced his body still. If he moved, the kid could get spooked. Even the smallest change of energy affected kids.

"That's okay," Brodey said, his voice somewhere between comforting and authoritative. "Do you think you've seen him?"

The kid's eyes bounced between Brodey and the sketch, but he backed up a step. "No."

From not being sure to no. This day was bringing all kinds of screwy surprises. As a cop, liars came in steady supply, including scared kids. What he had here might be both. The kid could be mentally reliving his father's murder in their home. No kid deserved to live with that mess.

Sam spun to his mom. "Can I go now?"

"Sam?" Brodey said.

"Yes, sir?"

"Are you sure you don't know him?"

"You know what," Brenda said, "they have homework to finish."

The kids left, their mother following them out, and the pressure behind Brodey's eyes exploded.

Brenda Williams, for whatever reason, suddenly didn't want her children asked any more questions.

Brodey held Lexi's briefcase while she unlocked her funky red front door. Only a decorator—scratch that, *interior designer*—painted the front door of a nine-hundred-square-foot bungalow glossy red. The place was begging to get knocked off. The bad outside lighting only added to the "rob me!" message.

"You know," he said, "the place could use better lightning. Especially if you do these late nights regularly."

"Seven-thirty is late?"

"It's dark, isn't it?"

She flipped the lock and pushed open the door. "You're funny, Brodey."

"I'm a cop who's seen women get mugged—

or worse—because they didn't take their surroundings seriously."

"I do take them seriously." Inside, she hit a switch and flooded the cottage with light. "But it's winter and there's only so much daylight. I can't avoid coming home after dark. Particularly when a cute homicide detective runs me all over town and my work doesn't get done. As it is, I had to cancel my last two appointments."

"Sorry about that. And I'm not cute. Men don't like to be called cute. Puppies are cute."

She dumped her briefcase by the door. "Fine. You're not cute. Tomorrow, though, I have to get moving on the Williams house. Are you going to let me tear up that laundry room?"

"You can't work around it?"

"Brodey!"

He put his hands up. "Just for a day or two."

"You've been over that place a million times. What will happen in a day or two that will make a difference?"

Hell if he knew. He *had* been over it from top to bottom, and everything he'd thought might tell him something—the slug in the wall, the broken glass, the open window—turned out to be nothing. No wonder the case was colder than Lake Michigan. Not one damned piece of workable evidence. And Lexi was on a deadline she intended to make.

"You can't tear it up. Yet."

She folded her arms, tapping her fingers against her biceps. "Forty-five days, Brodey. That's how long I have. And that's not to finish the renovation. That's for the house to sell. And the real-estate agent is calling me three times a day."

"Are you serious?"

"Yes, I'm serious. My voice mail was full today. Full. All clients wondering why I'm not responding. And this real-estate agent handles some megalistings. If I blow the deadline, I lose my chance at an assistant and, worse, my reputation. So, yes, handsome man, I need to rip that floor up."

Damn, she was beautiful. *No distractions here.* "Call me stupid, but I love when you get pushy like this. Makes me willing to give you just about anything."

"Great. Tomorrow the floor comes up."

"Except that."

Lexi burst out laughing. "I'm telling you straightaway, it will take a minor miracle to keep me from ripping up that floor."

She moved into the kitchen, grabbed two bottled waters from the fridge and set them on the counter separating the rooms. "Are you hungry? Earlier you promised me dinner and we haven't eaten since lunch."

Definitely, he could eat. Then again, he could always eat. "I'd love to buy you dinner."

"We can order something. All I have is chicken salad that might poison us. The Italian restaurant down the street delivers."

Her phone buzzed, rumbling against the countertop, where she'd set it. "Does that thing ever stop?"

"Only when I shut it off." She dug a menu out of the drawer and handed it to him. "Take a look. We'll order and then figure out what's next in your investigation."

He twisted his lips, perused the menu for all of two seconds. "Chicken parm. Spaghetti on the side."

"Good choice."

While she ordered, he scanned the stark-white counter, where a pitcher with splotches of color sat in one corner. Opposite that was a three-foot-high black vase with some kind of long-stemmed greenery poking out of it. Other than that, the counters were clear, no jumble of utensils, no appliances, no spice rack, nada. Everything in this kitchen had its place. Orderly.

Kind of like him, but he didn't want just order, he wanted control. Always.

Lexi set the phone down and immediately stored the menu back in the drawer. "Okay, handsome. We need a game plan here or I'm not getting the Williams house done. You've got two minutes to come up with something while I ditch my shoes. Then you'll tell me what we're doing about finding Ed Long."

She wandered to the other room. The bedroom. Unconcerned about her directive, he peeked around the column for a glimpse because, hey, the place wasn't that big and he was curious.

"I need to dig around," he said. "Figure out what the connection might be between Williams, Ed Long and Long's defense attorney. If we're going with Williams knowing his attacker, and Ed Long was that attacker, why was he in the Williams house the night of the murder? A guy like Williams wouldn't be hanging with someone like Long. There's a reason he was there. I may pay a visit to Henry again. Put a little pressure on him to see if he ever introduced them and why. He won't talk but I'll scare the hell out of him. He may be a defense lawyer, but he admitted he knew Williams. And Williams is definitely dead. Which doesn't look good for old Henry."

Lexi appeared in the bedroom doorway, her eyes huge, her mouth partially open. Every vibe coming off her screamed panic. What the hell?

"Lex?"

Eyes bugging out, she paddled her hands.

Pure and potent adrenaline spewed, tearing up his veins, making his stomach churn, and he hauled butt to the bedroom, gently nudging her from the doorway. "What?"

"The mirror. There."

She pointed to the stand-up mirror in the corner. Taped to it was one of the flyers she and Jenna had flooded Cartright with.

Another burst of adrenaline hit him and his vision blurred. He blinked it away and scanned the room, eyes sweeping left, right and back again. The top of the tall dresser held a few bottles of lotion and a couple of small glass bowls, all lined up like soldiers. Same thing with the long dresser, the two lamps and various decorative jars. Nothing out of place. "Did you tape that there?"

She'd damn well better say yes. If not, they had bigger problems than her needing more outside lighting.

"I DIDN'T PUT it there," Lexi said.

She stood in the doorway while Brodey studied the mirror, running the flashlight from his phone around the surface. Probably looking for fingerprints. A whirring noise drifted from the kitchen and Lexi glanced down the hall before moving closer to Brodey. She'd heard that refrigerator hundreds—thousands—of times and suddenly it terrified her?

Still, couldn't hurt to get closer to the trained police officer in the room. Yes. Good thought. "Do you see anything?"

"Maybe a print on the tape. You need to report it as a break-in. Is anything missing?"

Please, no. In her shock, she hadn't thought to check her belongings. Nothing looked out of place but...

She rushed to the dresser, riffled through the drawers where she'd strategically hid her quality jewelry—her grandmother's wedding ring, the diamond necklace she'd bought herself after her first big job, the heart earrings her father had given her. *Yes.* All items accounted for, she pushed the drawer closed and collapsed against the dresser, breathing in and out until her ears stopped their annoying whistling. "It's all here."

"You sure?"

"Yes. The important things are here."

Wedgwood vase. Would a petty thief know it was worth five thousand dollars? Another thing she hadn't paid for, but was given in exchange for the exposure offered from the design contest. She spun back, ran to the doorway and checked the side table in the tiny hallway. *Still there.* "That vase is the only other thing of value. Unless they wanted to carry the sofa out. Everything is here."

Except…she hadn't checked the top drawer. Her underwear drawer. She never kept anything important there, well, other than her underwear, but for the sake of completion, for the detail-oriented person in her who couldn't ignore the last drawer, she slid it open.

And oh no. Sitting in the middle, resting on top of her silk underwear, was another flyer. She focused on it, blinked away her blurry vision and read the words written in red ink across the top. Silently, she recited each word, letting her lips form them as they sunk in.

LEAVE.

THIS.

CASE.

ALONE.

In my house, in my house, in my house. "No," she moaned. "This is *not* happening."

Brodey leaped up, charged across the room and followed her gaze. He stared at the flyer a few seconds, then reached for his phone. "I'm calling it in. Don't touch that."

"You can bet I won't."

Not after some pig had put his hands on her things. Her extremely private things. Her stomach turned rock hard as Brodey spoke with a dispatcher and marched to the front door. Without touching it, he checked the lock, then went to the back door and did the same. She stood, half shivering, feet fused to the floor in the tiny hallway, watching him prowl around the house. All because she'd helped Jenna post those damned flyers. He'd warned her about this. Told her how dangerous it was. At the time, she'd considered him paranoid. A worrywart. Mr. Cynical.

Well, Mr. Cynical had nailed this one, and the caged panic inside her banged against her chest. Tears bubbled up—no crying—and she pressed her palms against her eyes.

Ending his call, Brodey reached for her, pulled her in for a hug and slid his hand over her hair. Mr. Touchy-Feely. Right now, she didn't mind. Not one bit.

"You're okay," he whispered, kissing the top of her head. "You're okay."

She gripped his shirt at his waist, drew in all his heat, praying it would douse the deep freeze that had settled inside her. "He was in my house."

"I know. I'm sorry. It doesn't look like he broke anything to get in. He probably picked the back-door lock. It's cheap. And useless."

"This had to be Ed Long. He was so creepy when he talked to me. It has to be him."

"You got someone's attention."

She tipped her head up to look at him. "Not any random person. Him. I know it. I can feel it."

"Or someone he knows. Could be someone he's working with."

In my house.

"They know where I live. They could be following me."

"Could be."

She shoved him back, flapped her arms. "You're not helping. You're supposed to make me feel better."

"By lying to you? By telling you not to worry when someone gets into your house and leaves you a threatening note? Not my style."

Mr. Cynical turning into Mr. Anti-Sensitivity. Killer combo, that one.

He latched on to her arms, gave them a squeeze. "I won't lie, but I promise—I swear to you—nothing will hurt you." He inched closer, still hanging on to her. "I'll make sure of it."

Of all the things men had told her over the years, for whatever reason, this might be the one she believed most. She imagined when Brodey Hayward, annoying as he was, made a promise, he kept it. She absorbed his words, took them in, once again silently repeating them over and over. After the third time, like a mantra, they settled the madness scouring her mind.

Relax. *You've got this.*

Brodey slid his hands to hers and grasped them. "Are you okay?"

Considering what had just happened and what *could* have happened had she walked in on the person? Yes. Absolutely okay. More than okay. Because her intruder wanted this, wanted her to give in to the fear. *Don't.* No. She lifted her head, imagined some stranger pawing through her possessions—her underwear—and suddenly her rock-hard stomach morphed into something else. Something loose and violent that tore up her insides in an angry, burning way.

She lifted his hand, kissed the back of it and held it to her cheek. "Thank you. For being here. Finding this alone would have been…"

"But you weren't alone, so don't go there."

Someone banged on the front door, devouring the silence and brief calm. Another surge of panic flooded her brain and she shot straight, her body in full alert.

"Relax," he said. "I've got it. It's probably a patrol car."

Chapter Nine

By the time the last police officer left, Lexi wanted nothing more than a hot bath, a full barrel of wine and to sleep for a month. When this mess began, she had dreams of an assistant. Her goals had been simple. Get the assistant, clean out the garage and make it an office. Now her privacy had been violated and her sense of safety right along with it. After putting so much energy into her home, endless hours of pouring herself into it, she wasn't sure she'd ever manage any sleep in it again.

All because she wanted an assistant.

She glanced around the living room, took in the red accents and the mint walls meant to bring tranquility. The camel chairs she'd spent so many nights sketching in, the sofa she'd prized to the point of worship. In a matter of hours, everything she felt about this home had changed.

She plopped onto one of the counter stools,

considered what had gone on here and shook her head, letting her festering rage burn into her. No one should be allowed to steal another person's sense of safety.

Brodey swung through the front door after talking with one of the officers outside. Now he bolted the door behind him and double-checked it.

"You know what?" she said.

"What?"

"I'm angry."

"You should be."

"A couple of hours ago, this house was my safe haven. Everything I've worked for is here. When the world is rotten, this is my shelter. And someone changed that. It's not right. I had to be *fingerprinted.*"

"It's only to rule out your prints."

"I know that, but the entire episode is unsettling."

"Well." He motioned one hand in circles. "Ah, hell. There's nothing to say. Yeah, it's unsettling. No two ways about it."

Finally, no lecture, no infinite wisdom on how to avoid something like this. *Thank you.*

He wandered to her, brushed a few stray strands of hair from her face, then set his big hand on her cheek. "You should feel violated.

I'll make sure it doesn't happen again. But you need to make changes around here."

Should have known. The man simply couldn't help himself. "Like what? Bars on the windows?"

"For one thing, motion-sensor lights by the front and back doors. Better locks, too. And you need a security system. Any single woman living alone should have one."

A security system. That would set her budget back, but feeling the way she did, her safety and sense of comfort compromised, whatever the cost, she'd accept it.

"I'll do it. No argument. Do you know a good security company?"

"I'll call a guy I know in the morning. I'm getting you lights with motion sensors, too. They'll be in by lunchtime."

"You can do that?"

He grinned. "I happen to be handy. Remember that when you think I'm driving you batty."

Parked on the stool, her life a wreck around her, she laughed. Straight from her toes it shot up and felt so darned good that she grabbed Brodey by the shirt and smacked a kiss on him. Just plastered her lips against his because if she'd been here alone, this situation would have been so much worse. He deepened the kiss and it became more than the quick smack she'd intended. His hands closed over her lower back and dragged her closer, their tongues clashing as he pushed between her legs. Oh my, this man could kiss.

He broke away, moving his lips along her jaw, dotting kisses until he got to her ear.

"I like kissing you," he whispered.

"I like you kissing me," she said.

He laughed and dropped his head to her shoulder. "Damn, you're great."

"But you stopped."

"Because we should get you settled for tonight before I beg to do dirty things to you. Why don't we move this to my place? It's a frat house compared with this, but you'll be safe there."

She hugged him, held him close, once again drawing in all that protective warmth. With Brodey came a sense of calm that anchored her, helped her stay in control.

Kept her sane.

Relatively.

She knew she wouldn't—couldn't—be chased from her home. If she gave in, her intruder won. And she refused to live that way. "I can't leave."

"Lex—"

"I've loved this cottage from the second I saw it. It has every piece of me I could give it. Whoever did this won't take that from me."

Brodey let out a breath, releasing the air

through his lips in one long flow. "I want to argue with you."

"But?"

"I get it. You don't deserve this. And it stinks. But you can't be alone until we get this place secure."

"Well," she said, suddenly feeling hopeful but maybe not quite ready to share a bed with a man, "*you* could stay here with me. I'll even give you the bedroom. I'll take the couch. Which is a major thing since I barely let anyone sit on it, much less put their feet on it."

"Hell no. I'll take the couch. You sleep in your bed and maybe it'll halfway feel like a normal night."

A normal night that included a break-in and a man who kissed like a demon sleeping on her twenty-thousand-dollar couch.

Sure.

Normal.

STARING AT LEXI'S living room ceiling at 2:00 a.m. stunk. Afraid to fall asleep, Brodey kept his mind sharp by doing math problems in his head. When that got old, he switched to the Williams case, methodically organizing a mental to-do list. He'd need to swing by Jenna's office and update her murder board. This thing was full of interesting angles, and laying it all out, seeing the flow, would help him build a solid theory. They had Ed Long pretending to live in Cartwright, possibly to get info out of Lexi. They had his number in the appointment book Lexi found buried in the wall. They had his lawyer knowing Jonathan Williams. How the hell did all this fit together?

"I need to check his financials," he said to no one.

Financials always told some sort of story. People were habitual with their spending. Whether a person was frugal or materialistic, a good detective could learn any number of things by simply studying bank records.

Moonlight filtered through a skylight in the kitchen, giving the place a terrific cozy feel. He could see why she loved it here. She'd built a home for herself, made it comfortable for anyone who walked in the door. When he'd told her his place looked like a frat house, he wasn't exaggerating. It came complete with milk crates as side tables. Maybe he'd have Lexi help him with it. Nothing crazy on his salary, but at least something that resembled an adult living there.

Footsteps in the hallway bolted him upright. He swung around and spotted Lexi in the hallway in a pair of silky-looking shorts and a V-neck top, her blond hair backlit by the moonlight. God, she looked great right out of bed. "You okay, Lex?"

In the darkness, her bare feet smacked lightly against the hardwood. "I'm fine. Restless. Did I wake you?"

He jammed his thumb and middle finger into his eyes for a good rub. "I was awake. Can't sleep."

"Me, neither. I hate it." She slid into the spot next to him and curled her legs under her. "Usually when I can't sleep, I come out here and work. Maybe do some sketches. It relaxes me."

"Work relaxes you?"

From his perspective, his job gave him nightmares.

"I guess with what you do, that sounds weird, but yes. I think it's more the quiet that comes with sketching rather than the actual activity. Although, there's something therapeutic in creating something with my own hands, watching it take shape."

"Uh, I can't draw a lick."

"So, don't draw. You said you're handy. Build model airplanes or something."

Brodey twisted his lips. That idea had possibilities. "Boats."

"What?"

He leaned back, bringing his bad arm up to rest it on the back of the couch. "I like boats.

When I retire, I want to be on the water. Maybe do fishing charters or something."

"From homicide to fishing?"

"Yep. And I'm moving someplace warm in the winter. I can't take this cold. I've got another fourteen and a half years and I'm done. Then I'll do something else."

She spun sideways, propped her arm on the cushion and her fingertips brushed his elbow. "You'd leave Chicago?"

"Only in the winter. My family is here. Besides, I love it here."

"I love it here, too. Unfortunately, my business doesn't allow me to pick up and go. Unless it's an out-of-state job. And what about kids? Do you want kids?"

He shrugged. "Never thought about it. Maybe."

"If you have kids, they'll be in school."

That was a problem he hadn't considered. Most likely because he hadn't met a woman who'd motivated him to think that far ahead.

At least not until now.

He tried to picture Lexi with a bun in the oven. His bun. Hello? A couple of kisses and a few laughs weren't nearly enough to build a family on. "You want kids?"

Using two fingers, she pressed on his hair. Probably the cowlick that sprang up every morning. "I think so. I'm a little old-fashioned, though, so I don't want to be a single mom. I guess if the right guy doesn't come along, I'd consider doing it myself, but right now, I'm okay to wait."

"Single parenting is tough. I don't think I could do it."

"Brodey, you can do anything you put your mind to. You're stubborn that way."

He snorted. "My mom says that."

"She must be a smart woman."

She'd like you. Yep. Sure would. His mom would like her spunk. *He* liked her spunk. He liked a lot about her. Particularly the way the moonlight lit enough of her for him to see her top dipping low into her cleavage—a nice view if he ever saw one. *No bra.* And that sent his mind spinning to thoughts of lifting the pajama top, running that silky fabric through his fingers and getting a look at her. He already knew her breasts were enough to fill a man's hand—his hand—nicely, but he'd never seen them. And that was what he wanted.

For safekeeping, he brought his arm down and clasped his fingers on his stomach. Thoughts of his hands on Lexi's breasts were trouble. Bigtime. His growing erection straining against his jeans proved it. Damn it.

"Did you fall asleep?"

Ha. "Hardly. In fact, I think it's safe to say I'm wide-awake."

"Why do I feel like I should apologize?"

He lifted his head, met her gaze, and that instant spark zapped him. So hot. "My mind wanders when I'm around you. Being here, in the dark, makes me think things. Seriously wicked things you'd slap me for."

A small intake of breath was her only response. He laid his head back again and sighed. *Moron.* What kind of man took advantage of a woman who'd had her safety, her sense of comfort in her own home, violated?

A horny one.

Sometimes, the truth stunk. He wanted to consider himself honorable, someone who wouldn't manipulate a situation to reach the conclusion he wanted. As a detective, he battled tunnel vision and that driving need to solve a case at all costs. A good detective worked with the evidence he had, made it fit, and sometimes, despite honest intentions, that evidence added up to convicting the wrong person.

She lowered her head to his shoulder. Definitely not slapping him. Maybe he wasn't such a lowlife.

"What kind of things?"

Man, oh, man. The living room was definitely warming up.

"Lex?"

She lifted her head, met his gaze. "Yes?"

"You're about to throw a match on leaking gas."

"I know. I've been alone a while and it's a little scary to me—this attraction to you."

He reached up, tucked his hand behind her head and pulled her closer. Even in the darkness, her hazel eyes were bright, charged with something resembling anticipation.

Waiting.

Damn, they weren't exactly perfect for each other. She viewed the world with a sense of innocence, wanting only to make it more beautiful. Him? All he saw was what could happen. The danger that existed the minute she stepped out of her house. The danger that now made its way *inside* her house.

But he wanted her.

Simple as that.

Then she made a humongous mistake by leaning in, enough that her breath skittered across his cheek and—*man down*—any motivation he had to stop flew out the window. Right out. *Bye-bye*.

"There are a million reasons we're wrong for each other," he said.

She slid her hand over his chest, between his pecs, and the friction ripped right into him. He should give in now because it had been too long since he'd had a woman, and this wasn't just any woman. This amazing, beautiful, sassy woman he'd like to hear moaning underneath him. At least when his damned elbow healed since he couldn't put any weight on it. *Way to kill the mood.*

"I think you're wrong about that," she said. "Besides, do we care right now? Clearly, we're attracted to each other. I mean, I'm not great with men, but that smoking kiss was a good indication, don't you think?"

A good indication.

So much for honorable. Brodey gave his head a hard shake. He didn't know what the hell he wanted. No. That was a lie. He knew. He just didn't want to give in to it. And how dumb was that? They were adults, reasonable adults— mostly—who wanted to have some fun.

Fun. That was what they'd have.

And while he did all this thinking, the furnace clunked, driving even more heat into the already boiling room while she straddled him.

"I like to think I'm a fairly confident person, but this is starting to feel like a rejection. You've got ten seconds to kiss me before I give up on you. And, Brodey, when I give up on a man, it's over. No going back."

As proved by her walking away from the cheating ex.

Couldn't have that, could they?

He slid his hands around her waist, settled them on her hips where his fingers hit bare skin at the bottom edge of her top. His blood raced and he breathed in, enjoyed the sensation of his skin against hers. He curved his hands over her rear, inching along because why not? Putting his hands on her was the thing he'd been craving for days.

"I hope you're not tired," he said.

"Why?"

"Because you're about to have a long night."

LEXI SQUEEZED HER thighs against Brodey's and her legs tingled with each bit of contact. She'd missed that feeling. The anticipation. The *lust*. "Bring it on, fella."

She lowered her head to kiss him, but he was already in motion, pulling her in, and then her lips were on his, raking against them, nipping and sucking and…crazy good. A fierce buzz roared inside her, tearing straight up into her breasts and—wow—this kiss. Too much. Too. Much.

Never before had she thrown herself at a man. Never. They always came to her. With Brodey, she didn't need him to chase her. She simply knew what she wanted. Somewhere along the way, he'd given her reasons to trust him. The way he watched over her, protected her, listened to her. All of it brought safety. Emotionally and physically.

Even if the man drove her insane. Which he was about to do on her treasured sofa.

In a grand way.

He dug his hands under her shirt, slid the hem up, his roughened fingers scorching over her skin. "Get it off."

Together, eyes locked, they worked the fabric over her head and tossed it on the floor. Her own little striptease. She took a second to absorb the fact that she was almost fully naked—tap pants still firmly in place—and he hadn't removed a stitch of clothing.

She kissed him again, pressing against him and reveling in the light abrasion of his shirt against her bare skin. "You have too many clothes on."

Then she was airborne as he shifted her sideways. "I can fix that."

The two of them went to work on his clothes, him removing his shirt while she worked on his zipper. The shirt gone, he grabbed his wallet from the arm of the sofa. Before tonight, that wallet sitting there, disturbing the order, possibly leaving smudges on the fabric, would have grated her nerves. Now? Who cared? He pulled something from the wallet. Condom. Good thinking.

He boosted his hips and she glided his jeans down, hooking her fingers into his boxer briefs, bringing them along with the jeans. Multitasking at its best.

His erection sprang free and Lexi figured she'd just hit the lottery of male perfection. She skittered her fingers over his legs, good solid legs a woman could count on to hold her up. He stepped out of his jeans and she tossed them aside, then stood in front of him, running her hands along the ridges of his stomach, up his chest and—dear God, the man was all lean, sinewy muscle. This was a body toned and carved to perfection.

"Lex?"

"Yes?"

"Uh, there's one thing."

Of course there was. The man had a lecture for everything. Forget that. She dived into his neck, trailing kisses up and up and up, along his jaw, to his lips, and he set her back a step.

"Brodey, I love this protective streak in you and how you worry about every darned thing, but you can stop now. Please."

"I'm sorry, but…"

Enough. She lurched back. Might as well just

let him say what he needed to say and they could get down to business. "What is it?"

He stuck his elbow out. "Bum arm."

She burst out laughing. "And that's a problem now?"

"Uh, yeah."

"I don't understand."

He grunted. "I can't believe you're gonna make me say it."

As the seconds ticked by, tension mounted and her brain hit overdrive—*what am I missing? What's he worried about?* No idea. Using her palm, she banged on her forehead. "I don't know what you're trying to say."

"Lex! I can't put any weight on my arm. You have to do the work."

Say what now?

Again, he held his elbow up and the look on his face, the pressed lips, the scrunched nose, all of it a cross of frustration, humiliation and sheer will. She grabbed his cheeks and dotted kisses over his face. "It's okay, it's okay. I get it now."

"It's not okay. I should be able to hold up my own damned weight."

More kisses. "You can. Just not right now. It's okay. Really." She shoved him backward until the backs of his legs hit the sofa and he dropped onto it. "Lucky for you, I like being on top."

He smiled at her joke. Mission complete.

Gone was the frustration and embarrassment. The vulnerability. From a man who'd never shown her any sign of weakness. *I could love him.*

But she wouldn't go to that particular place. That meant risking heartbreak. For now, she'd focus on the lust that, after months and months without it, brought her alive again. She stood in front of Brodey, watching him tear the condom wrapper, anticipating that second when he'd be ready and she'd pounce—literally—on him.

She waggled her hand. "Seriously? How long does it take? Should I do it?"

He snorted. "*No.* Sheesh, someone's in a rush." *You know it, mister.*

He held his arms wide. "Come and get me."

Then she was on him and a frenzy of kisses and licking and touching ensued. Neck, shoulders, jaw, everywhere. *Poof.* Total combustion. Insanity.

Loving the feel of his skin against hers, that rub of flesh against flesh, she inched closer, craving that first second when he'd be inside her, filling her. He gripped her hips and—*finally*—she gasped at the intrusion. So long she'd been without this.

He stopped. "You okay?"

"I'm great. Keep moving or I'll kill you. Right on my sofa."

The one she barely let anyone sit on.

She rolled her hips and he moaned, a low, guttural sound that melted her mind.

They moved together and her body became a tight coil, waiting, waiting, waiting. *Please.* So perfect. How was it possible he felt this perfect? This right.

Kidding herself.

Struck stupid by lust. Had to be.

Did she care? *No.*

He bucked his hips and her breath hitched. Something bright and sharp and beautiful flashed behind her eyes. *I could love him.* Her body exploded, just came apart bit by bit, and she cried out, hanging on as he moved inside her. She grabbed his cheeks and held on, wanting to see his face when he went over.

Gritting his teeth, he took a sharp breath as his orgasm hit him full force. He tightened his arms around her, bringing her with him as he slumped back against the sofa. So good together. Who knew? The cynical cop and the hopeful designer. What a team. Snuggling in, she rested her head against his chest, where his heartbeat thump-thumped in her ear. Slowly, she twirled her fingers in the smattering of dark hair, enjoying the silence and the odd familiarity, the comfort, that shouldn't come from a man she'd slept with only once.

Comfort and familiarity that she'd experienced only one other time, with someone who'd humiliated her with his intern.

Don't think about it. The hurt and anger and unwillingness to take a chance on someone.

Not now. Not when she'd finally found a man who wouldn't lie to her or keep secrets.

One she might trust.

FOR THE FIRST time in months, Brodey woke up thinking he'd not only hit the lottery, he'd also hit the sex-all-night *mega*lottery, and in his mind, that was one hell of a way to start the day.

Even if he was dog tired.

He pried his eyes open, blinked a few times and focused on the weird color of Lexi's bedroom ceiling. Why the hell would anyone paint a ceiling peach? Then again, why would anyone pay twenty grand for a couch?

He didn't get it.

Lexi's world was an enigma. An enigma he'd have to start understanding if he expected a woman like her to continue playing the megalottery with him.

But, damn, her world was all happy, calm colors, while his was dark crime. She saw light where he saw gloom. Eventually, his need to point out the obvious dangers and her need to ignore him would blow any relationship to bits.

Next to him, Lexi flopped to her stomach, her sandy-blond hair splaying over her pillow. Immediately, thoughts of nudging her awake and really giving this day a bang of a start filled his mind. He considered it. Sure did. But as tired as he was, she had to be just as tired and had clients to see today. At least he could nap.

He stared back up at the ceiling, tilted his head one way, then the other. Oddly, his already supremely under-control blood pressure dropped another notch. Huh. Maybe she had something with all this feng shui nonsense. He closed his eyes, thought about the day ahead. After last night's break-in and the subsequent call to the PD, he needed to come clean to his superiors about his involvement investigating this case. He was a cop and cops talked and before he knew it, the brass would want answers.

Plus, he needed help. After the warning left for Lexi, he couldn't investigate and keep her safe at the same time.

Hold up here, bud.

His superiors? Was that necessary? They didn't know the case, at least not the intricacies, the nuts and bolts. Not as well as the lead detective. And that guy was a friend of his father's. Brodey could head in there, turn over any evidence he and Lexi had found and tell the detective to help himself to the credit. Brodey's name wouldn't even have to come up.

This might be a plan.

Slowly, he folded the sheet and bedspread back and slid out of bed. The sudden chill bolted right into his feet. Damned winters. A hot shower would do him some good. Help run the morning kinks out of his elbow. He'd help himself to that, head for clean clothes and call his father to hang with Lexi while he went to the PD and confessed his sins.

Chapter Ten

Brodey stood in reception at Area North headquarters waiting for Detective Lawrence McCall to answer his page. A woman sat to his left, her head buried in some kind of needlepoint project, and a sudden punch of yearning blasted him, ate right through his core. Who would expect to see a woman doing needlepoint in a police station? A cop. That was who. Because cops saw oddball stuff every day and that part of the job kept him sane, gave him something to laugh about after seeing things no right-minded human should.

"Junior!" McCall's booming voice echoed against the walls.

The man stood at the door leading into the main area of the building, his big chest stretching his dress shirt to barely bursting, and Brodey thought maybe the guy had lost some weight. He also wore a snarky grin. Old-timers like Larry, guys who couldn't understand why female detectives didn't want to be referred to as *broads*,

knew being called Junior broke Brodey's chops.
In a bad way.

"Lawrence," Brodey said, loading him up on
the sarcasm, "how's it going?"

McCall snorted. *Yeah, you're not the only one
who can bust chops.* When Dad had arrived at
Lexi's, he'd given Brodey inside information
that as a child, McCall was often teased about
being a nerd whose mother called him Lawrence instead of the shortened Larry. At times,
the guys around the station liked to crawl under
the man's skin by calling him Lawrence.

McCall whapped him on the back of the head
and shoved him through the door with a laugh.
"How you been? Everything okay? Your dad
told me about the elbow."

"I'm good. Don't start with the elbow jokes.
I'm out of my freaking mind with boredom."

McCall gestured down the long corridor.
"Who'd have thought you'd miss this job, right?"

"Amen, brother."

"What are you doing here?"

"It's about one of your cases. You got somewhere we can talk?"

McCall flopped his bottom lip out. "Sure."

He led him down the corridor to an empty
interview room where the ripe, stagnant smell
of sweat and fear permeated the air. Thousands
of people had sat through questioning in here,

some guilty, some not. But one thing was for sure—when they entered this room, their central nervous systems reacted. And not in a good way.

Brodey dropped his messenger bag on the floor. The bag contained his notes, Lexi's flyer and a sketch of Long that he'd be turning over to McCall. He parked himself in one of the metal chairs bracketing the table and tension sped up his arms like swarming spiders, their tiny legs powering along. He cupped a hand over the back of his neck and rubbed. How the heck had he'd gotten himself into this mess? All he'd wanted to do was kill a day by helping his sister.

McCall scraped the chair against the linoleum, and the sharp sound drove into Brodey's skull. Or maybe that was just his nerves.

"So, what's up?"

Making direct eye contact, Brodey eased his shoulders back. Command presence, the ability to look confident and in control, sometimes meant the difference between bleeding out in the street or making a bust.

"The Williams case."

"My nightmare. What about it?"

"I have information. All I ask is that you hear me out."

The detective dropped his chin to his chest and groaned. "Ah, Junior, what the hell's this, now?"

"Nothing horrible." Brodey waggled a hand. "It's good. But my butt could wind up in a sling."

"Start talking, kid."

"You know my sister is an investigator for Hennings & Solomon."

"You better believe I know. She's too damned good at her job and wrecks my cases."

Brodey smiled. "I hear you. She's been volunteered by her boss to help Brenda Williams figure out what happened to her husband."

"Damn it."

He didn't know the half of it. "She asked me to take a look at her evidence. Couldn't make sense of a few things."

McCall made hard eye contact. "Junior, are you gonna upset me?"

Probably, but Brodey blew that off, just kept right on talking. "I took a look at the crime scene."

He'd casually leave out that his father had gotten him copies of the reports without McCall's knowledge. The thing with old-timers was to dazzle them, not give them a chance to pound on you before you got to the good stuff.

"And?"

"There's a guy. Ed Long. You know him?"

Slowly, McCall moved his head back and forth, his cheeks tinting red, but so far, no major tantrum. Brodey reached into his messenger bag for Lexi's sketch and his file on Long. "This is him. He's got a sheet. Mostly robberies. No murders."

"How does he tie back to Williams?"

"Mrs. Williams wants to unload their house. She's broke and needs the cash. She hired a decorator to stage the house, you know, make it look good so it'll sell faster. The decorator was approached by this Ed Long outside the house, started asking her questions."

McCall screwed up his face. "And what? He introduced himself? Gave her his name?"

"Hell no. That's where it gets good."

Brodey spent the next ten minutes walking McCall through how he and Lexi learned Ed Long's identity. When he finished, McCall picked up the sketch, compared it with the photo of Long from his rap sheet.

"The link between Williams and this Long guy is the lawyer?"

"I think so. The lawyer's kid went to school with Williams's kid."

"So what? How does that tie Long to Williams?"

"I don't know. But someone broke into Lexi Vanderbilt's house last night and left one of the flyers with a note telling her to back off."

That got McCall's attention. "Hell no."

"Hell yes. I was there with her."

"Why?"

Why? Dummy him hadn't anticipated that question, and he should have. Any good detective would. "I had follow-up questions about her conversation with Long, so I went over there. She found the note while I was there." As recoveries went, that one wasn't half-bad. "Obviously, I called it in. The crime-scene guys took the note to check it for prints."

"And you're coming to me now because you're on disability and might get jammed up."

"For the record, this was supposed to be a one-day thing. I'd give Jenna my opinion. That's all. She's my baby sister and she was stuck."

Working McCall's soft spot as a family man, another inside tip from Dad, couldn't hurt.

The big man snorted. "Your father prepped you. So far, you've worked my nerves with the Lawrence crack and sucked up by mentioning your family. You're a kid after my own heart."

Brodey waggled his eyebrows. "I'm trying."

"But you're messing with my case." He mashed his finger into the table. "I want Jenna's evidence. Make that happen and I don't jam you up with the brass."

For Brodey, that worked. He'd have a not-so-happy Jenna to deal with, but his sister would agree if it kept Lexi out of danger. When it came to people's lives, the Haywards didn't mess around.

And, hey, if all else failed, guilt, in his family, was an intoxicating drug. If things went sideways, his involvement with the Williams case could wreck his career, and he'd damn sure use it to get his sister's cooperation.

"Fine," Brodey said. "I can take you to Hennings & Solomon. That's where her notes are. There's one thing."

"What?"

"We need to look at the Williamses' and Ed Long's bank statements. Ed Long is broke. He skipped out on his landlord last month. So, he's either run out of money or never had any in the first place."

McCall sat back, rested his hands on his belly and eyeballed Brodey. The man had been doing this job long enough to follow the trail of Brodey's thoughts. Whether he agreed with those thoughts would soon make itself evident.

"You got a set of stones, kid. You bust in on my case and now you're thinking the wife may have something to do with this—like we didn't already work that angle? Well, genius, we did. We cleared her."

"I know you did."

"But you're gonna break chops about it. Like I haven't been doing this thirty-five years? Like I'm some baby detective who can't find the john on his own?"

Guys like McCall, any detective really, didn't want to be second-guessed by younger, slicker detectives who went to college, who got their starts by studying criminal behavior in a classroom rather than on the street. Brodey met his gaze straight on. Showing any signs of intimidation would absolutely give McCall power. And Brodey didn't give away power. "All due respect, I'm coming to you. Telling you what we've found. And yes, confirming a few things. This is a cold case. An unsolved murder. I don't think kicking the tires a second time hurts. But that's up to you. It's your case skewing the city's unsolved violent crime stats."

Brodey stood. He'd said his piece. If McCall wanted to ignore what he'd found, that was his problem. It would eat Brodey alive, tear at him like acid in his gut, but he'd walk away. He had to. Now that he'd admitted working the case, he'd have to back off or be subject to sanctions when McCall went to the higher-ups.

But Brodey wouldn't leave this alone. Not completely. His sister was a skilled investigator. He'd stay in the background, advising her until they busted Ed Long and possibly Brenda Williams. Lexi he'd have to keep close, make sure she stayed safe. After last night, a damned fine option.

Right now, sitting in this interview room,

despite a beefy, hardened detective—damn, he didn't want to be this guy in thirty years—trying to aggravate him, Brodey's life didn't stink.

"What's the matter, Junior? You gonna take your ball and go home?"

Thirty years.

A stream of mental curses he'd love to unleash banged around in his head. *Stay calm.* Once again, he set his shoulders. "That's the thing, McCall. It's not my ball. It's yours."

Bang. The detective flew out of his chair, his face hurtling beyond crimson and landing on blue.

"What?" Brodey said. "You're gonna take a swing at me? That'll be easy to explain."

The big man halted, literally skidding to a stop as his reality took hold. He had an unsolved case, new leads provided by a detective who shouldn't be anywhere near said case, and now he wanted to bust that detective up. Truth be told, the guy was big enough to pummel Brodey. He'd give him a go, make McCall work up a sweat and maybe get a few good licks in, but the bum elbow wouldn't help and he'd wind up with a whupping.

But McCall unclenched his fists, backed up three steps, and the redness in his face, all that surging blood, drained. Within seconds, his color reached the pasty white that came with a Chicago winter.

Or years as a homicide detective.

McCall leaned against the wall, crossed his arms and contemplated the floor. "You really boxed me in, didn't you, Hayward?"

Again, the hardened detective's ego had him veering toward the negative. *I don't want to be this guy.* If this was what thirty-five years on the job did to a man, Brodey would be taking Lexi's advice and finding a hobby. Fast.

"I don't see it that way, McCall. If Ed Long is a murderer, I helped you solve your case. Do you have the financial records?"

"Of course I do."

"Then let's start there. See if there's a money trail."

LEXI UNLOCKED THE front door on the Williamses' home and strode inside. Behind her, Brodey's father carried two sample books in each hand, saving her a second trip to her car. This would be life with an assistant. She couldn't wait. A helper and a fellow creative to bounce ideas off of, to sketch with, to plan with. They'd work side by side building her—their—business together. In a few years, Lexi wanted to see her name among the top five designers in Chicago—maybe in the *country*. Why not? Talent, hard work and the right assistant would get her there.

First, she needed to get this house done so the real-estate agent could sell it in time for her to get her bonus. Without the bonus, there'd still be an assistant—and an office—it just wouldn't happen for another six months. In which time, she might collapse from lack of sleep, fall into a lifelong coma and never have sex with Brodey Hayward again. And that might be the biggest tragedy of it all.

"Ew," she said.

Mr. Hayward swung the sample books onto the kitchen's center island. "What happened?"

"Nothing. I was thinking."

About comas. And world-class sex with your son. A burst of heat shot into her breasts because—thank you, thank you—Brodey Hayward was an ace in bed. He'd managed to light up every inch of her body, something she'd never experienced before and wanted plenty more of.

I need that assistant. Without the assistant, her Brodey time wouldn't happen. Particularly when he went back to work. Assuming he wanted to continue spending time with her. Maybe one night was all he'd wanted and now they were done.

Nah.

Sure didn't seem that way.

And wasn't this *exactly* what she didn't want in her life? When she'd walked out of her ex-fiancé's office, she vowed to never invest that much of herself in another person again. In the beginning with him, she thought she'd had it all. A rising superstar in the financial world, a caring, patient man who understood her and her business. Instead, she got a person who kept her up at night worrying over silly and not-so-silly things. A person she loved enough that it drove her to debilitating stomach issues when he'd betrayed her, a person so selfish that he'd left his damned office door unlocked while he had *sex* with his *intern* on his desk.

Moron.

Life this past year had been busy, and maybe a little lonely, but when she managed to sleep, she did it like a champ. Every night when she finally dropped into bed, whether from exhaustion or her solitary life where she didn't concern herself with a mate, she passed right out.

A voice—Mr. Hayward—pulled her from her stupor and she spun back to him, this man whose son had his emerald eyes and dark hair. The build was all wrong, though. Brodey was taller, leaner where his father had bulk. Oh, she needed to get Brodey out of her head and get some work done. "I'm sorry. I didn't hear you."

He pointed to the laundry room. "Is this the room?"

The murder room. "Yes. You know, your son is quite stubborn. He won't let me rip up the floor."

Mr. Hayward grinned. "That's my boy. Stubborn and conscientious."

"Which I think is wonderful. But I have work to do. If there's still evidence in there, we need to collect it so I can get to work."

"You want me to talk to him?"

Somehow she didn't think Brodey would appreciate his father running interference between them. An alpha through and through, he'd want to deal with her directly. "No. I'll talk to him. But thank you."

Leaving her standing at the center island, Mr. Hayward checked out the laundry room. He reached in, flipped on the light.

"What's this box?"

A box? When she'd left yesterday, the room had been empty. Nate. Could be he dropped supplies off. She wandered to the doorway. In the middle of the room sat a cardboard box, roughly fifteen inches all around. The top flaps where interlaced but unsealed.

Two things immediately registered. One, if these were supplies, the box was in awfully good shape for Nate's standards, and two, the amount of tile they needed for this room wouldn't fit inside a box that size.

"Lexi?"

"It's not mine. It could be supplies from my contractor."

"But you don't think so."

She met his gaze and a nasty, sour taste poured into her mouth. "No. I don't think so."

"I'll open it. See what's what."

"Wait. Should we call the police? What if it's…"

What? *A bomb.*

Was she turning into Brodey now with worry and paranoia ruling her life? Still, after finding the flyer in her house last night, anything would be possible.

As if she were some feebleminded civilian, Mr. Hayward tilted his head, his face a cross between pity and amusement. "And if it's supplies from the contractor?"

That would be her luck. The first time ever she suffered a bout of paranoia and it could be paintbrushes. "You're right. I'm sorry. A little jumpy I guess. I blame this on your son. Before I met him, I wasn't paranoid. He's a maniac, you know."

Mr. Hayward smiled that same lightning-quick and incredibly charming smile Brodey liked to hit her with. "Maybe. But he's also a cop. A damned good one. You want to wait outside while I check this box?"

She sure did. But no, as with the note left in her home the night before, she refused to give in and run from her life. "No. I'll stay."

Squatting next to the box, he checked it from different angles, not speaking a word. Listening maybe? She didn't know. Did bomb timers even tick anymore? Weren't they all digital? Again with the paranoia about ticking bombs.

It paid off, though. By the time she refocused on Mr. Hayward, he had the flaps of the box open. For a few seconds he remained silent and Lexi studied the back of his head, where wisps of gray mixed with his dark hair. "What is it?"

"A blanket."

Now, that was weird. Who would leave a blanket in the middle of the laundry room? And why? She wandered over and peered over Mr. Hayward's shoulder. A flash of faded red caught her eye and she studied the two-inch trim. The patchwork. The flashes of pink here and there.

She gasped, holding her breath until her chest ached, and Mr. Hayward spun back to her.

"What is it?"

"That quilt."

"You recognize it?"

"It's my grandmother's. It should be on the shelf in the back of my closet."

Chapter Eleven

"You got here at what time?"

Brodey stood in the Williamses' laundry room, hands on hips, mind absolutely disintegrating, while his dad explained to him and McCall how the quilt was discovered. Thirty minutes ago, he'd been in an interrogation room sorting through financials and now—boom— he had another problem.

And it was a big one.

"Around ten forty-five," Dad said. "I opened the box at ten-fifty. I checked the time."

McCall moved to the door leading outside. Hands on his knees, he bent low to inspect the lock. Lexi scooted beside Brodey, arms folded, fingers digging into her blazer with enough force to practically protrude through the material. From his vantage point, her entire body appeared stiff. As much as she tried to soften her facial features, the sucked-in cheeks were a dead giveaway of the tension paralyzing her body.

He set his hand on her shoulder only to have her flinch in return. "You okay?"

"All I did was hang a few flyers and call that damned phone number. Why is this person harassing me? I mean, he broke into my house, stole my quilt and brought it here for me to find? Why?"

Whoever this was—and Brodey was pretty damned sure it was Ed Long—was in panic mode. For whatever reason, he'd fixed on Lexi as the one reigniting this case and aimed to terrify her enough to get her to back off.

"Because he can," Brodey said.

"I didn't even realize the quilt was gone."

"Lex, it was only last night."

"Still. I should have checked the closet. I checked everything else."

"Give yourself a break. I didn't check the closet, either. And I'm a cop."

McCall finished inspecting the lock.

"Anything?" Brodey asked.

"Nah."

"So how'd they get in? All the windows locked?"

His father nodded. "Checked 'em all."

"Which leaves the possibility that someone had a key."

Lexi's mouth dropped open, her face stretching long. "Like Nate? Or Brenda? Stop it."

"Hey." He waved one hand. "You want to walk around in your the-world-is-beautiful utopia, knock yourself out. But my guess is it would take a helluva lock picker to handle these locks. Maybe that's the case, but I doubt it. If the locks weren't picked and the windows are intact, someone got in here using a key."

"Brodey, you can be a jerk sometimes."

Great. Name-calling. "Why? Because I can't drill it into your head that sometimes people you think are innocent aren't? That people you trust shouldn't be trusted? You, of all people, should know that."

The minute—no, the second—it came out of his mouth, he regretted it. And by the stunned look on her face, those big hazel eyes so wide, he knew the arrow had hit its mark. She'd confided in him, trusted him with the fact that her ex-fiancé had betrayed her, and Brodey had just used it against her. Yeah, he could be a jerk sometimes.

"Like I said, *Detective*, you can be a jerk sometimes."

Completely aware that his father and McCall were dialed in and waiting for the next round, he held up his hands. No sense giving them a show. His father he didn't mind. He told him everything anyway. McCall? He didn't necessarily know him. Didn't necessarily trust him, either. "I'm sorry. That was a cheap shot."

"Ya think?"

Venom—pure and deadly—glistened in Lexi's eyes. Ms. The-World-Is-a-Beautiful-Place had a temper. "Lex—"

"Oh, Brodey. Just shut up. You've said enough."

All at once, his father let out a low whistle and McCall cleared his throat. Brodey had to laugh. Yes, indeed, quite a show. Time to get this conversation back on track. Later, he'd talk to Lexi, find a way to apologize for being a world-class moron. He turned to McCall. "You need to take this quilt into evidence."

"I'll get the crime-scene people in here and do a supplement to the report from Lexi's place last night. Did you get the badge number of the cop who responded?"

"Yeah." Brodey dug into his pocket for his notepad. "683. Ericson."

"All right. I'll get a hold of him and add this." McCall shrugged. "Who knows, maybe we'll get some DNA or fibers."

Off to the side, Lexi shifted. "What happens then?"

"Then," Brodey said, "we hope like hell we get a hit on DNA from the night of the murder."

THE SECURITY SYSTEM was in.

Lexi curled her lip at the ugly keypad disrupting the flow of energy to the left of the doorway.

All that time spent sampling paint colors and that eyesore had just wrecked her wall. She'd have to come up with a way to cover the nasty-looking thing. Make it more unobtrusive and perhaps use a hinged frame to hide it.

As if it sensed her negative opinion regarding its appearance, the keypad beeped. Actually, it was more of a shrill, earsplitting whine.

Dear.

God.

Brodey stopped pushing buttons and glanced at her. "Are you paying attention?"

To the sqwauking, yes. His activity, not so much. She shook it off. "I got distracted. Sorry. Can we change the tone of the beep?"

"I know you hate this. But it's important."

"Just keep reminding me of that."

"I said you could come to my place."

"No. This is my home. I'm not running from it." She gestured to the keypad. "Show me again how to use this beast."

Five minutes later, he'd reviewed all the buttons on the keypad and gave her a cheat sheet of the codes. One for motion detection, one for glass break, one for both. All of it was too much.

"I think I've got it. As loud as that beep is, I certainly won't forget to disarm the system when I come in."

What she needed now was food and a glass

of wine. After this day, maybe she'd take the bottle. Seven o'clock and she'd just realized she'd skipped lunch. By the time they'd gotten through at the Williamses' home, she was dangerously close to running late for her afternoon appointments and gobbled a handful of cashews she'd found in a bag at the bottom of her purse. From the look of the tattered bag, they'd been there awhile. She'd eaten them with gusto, though. What a life.

And they still hadn't talked about their little tiff today.

Wow. That Brodey knew how to deliver a zinger. Between the overbearing protectiveness and the constant lecturing, he was far from perfect. But, unfortunately, part of her loved that about him and it made it hard for her to stay mad. After all, there were worse things than having a man worry about her. Considering the last man in her life never did—on any level.

Brodey's expertly delivered zinger had stunned and hurt her, but at least he'd recognized it and apologized. She looked over at him. "I want to talk about what happened today."

"Good. Me, too. I was wrong. Too wound up and I took it out on you."

"I didn't like it."

He nodded. "As soon as I said it, I knew I screwed up." He rubbed his hands over his face, held them there a second before dragging them away. "You scare the hell out of me. I don't think you sense danger when you should."

"And I think you sense danger when you shouldn't. Maybe that comes from being raised by someone in law enforcement and then seeing it firsthand, but I am who I am, Brodey. And I have no desire to change. If I wanted to see the world the way you do, I'd become a cop. Simple as that."

"I'm sorry. It won't happen again."

Easily, she could continue this conversation and pound on him more, but really…not her style. He'd apologized and admitted his mistake. That alone was worth something. A lot of men would have attempted to justify their actions. Make her question herself. Not Brodey. He owned it.

"Thank you," she said. "Are you hungry?"

He angled his head, squinted a little. "That's it?"

"I said what I needed to."

"Huh."

"This may shock you, but I have no interest in making this a world crisis. It happened, you apologized, we move on." She grinned in that tight way people did when sarcasm was needed. "I hardly think that transgression requires me to banish you from my life."

"Thank you. And, for the record, I think you're amazing. I'd have definitely made me suffer longer."

"Yeah, well, remember this moment when I do something you don't agree with." She swirled her hands. "Come to the dark side, Brodey, and see the world with rose-colored glasses. You might like it."

He laughed. So did she, and the misery of the day suddenly didn't seem so bad. Being mad at him took too much energy and zapped her creatively. All of her afternoon appointments had been a struggle. She'd managed a few good ideas, but not nearly her best work. She'd make it up to the clients. Without a doubt, her next ideas and sketches had to be spectacular.

Even if it killed her.

"So," she said, "I need food. You?"

"Starved."

"I'll order us a pizza. I like veggie."

"You're joking, right?"

She laughed. God, she loved how he made her laugh. "I wish you could see your face right now. No. I'm not joking. I like veggie pizzas. No meat. If you want meat I'll get two smalls."

"I don't mind the veggies, but you sure as hell need some meat on there. Get me a supreme."

"Ew. Hope you weren't planning on kissing me tonight."

"Honey, I'm planning on doing a whole lot more than kissing you."

And oh my, that sounded promising. "I guess we'll see about that."

He dropped onto her sofa and tossed his messenger bag on the coffee table. "After you order, wanna help me look at the Williamses' bank statements? You've got the eye for detail."

Lexi ordered their pizza, poured two glasses of wine and joined Brodey on the sofa. "You do drink wine, don't you?"

So much she needed to learn about this man.

"I'm more of a beer guy, but wine is good, too."

"Got it. I'll add it to the list."

The carefully arranged photography books were moved off the coffee table and set on the floor. A week ago, she'd have gutted him for disturbing the balance of her carefully crafted room. Now? After all he'd done, she'd suck it up and allow him these minor intrusions. As long as it didn't include breaking her heart. That, he was not allowed to do.

He spread the statements across the bare surface of the table and snap, snap, snapped his fingers in front of her face. "I'm losing you again."

"No. You're not." She nudged him with her elbow. "That time I heard you. We're looking for a break in the pattern. Anything that looks odd."

"Correct. I looked at these this morning, but didn't have time to study them. McCall told me Williams moved money a lot. He constantly played with his own portfolio. You'll see all the transfers."

Lexi scanned the rows of numbers on one statement then moved to the next…and the next. *Holy moneybags.* Page after page indicated tens of thousands of dollars randomly withdrawn from the accounts.

"Wow," she said.

"Yep. He kept a money-market account he parked cash in every month. If they ran low, he or Brenda—she was a cosigner—would move funds from the money market into their checking account. He liked to have a minimum of twenty grand liquid at all times."

"Nice slush fund."

Someday she'd have that slush fund. Unlike Jonathan Williams, she'd use it for security purposes. To make sure the mortgage and bills were paid.

"Sometimes," Brodey said, "the amounts varied from five hundred to thousands of dollars. We don't know how much of that money, considering the Feds were investigating him, was his own."

He pushed one of the reports away and slouched next to her, resting his head back.

Eyes narrowed in concentration, he appeared focused and—well—male. Incredibly, beautifully male. She'd love to sketch him at this moment, capture the intensity, the curve of his jaw, his straight, sculpted nose, his lightly curling hair. Not in this lifetime would she call Brodey Hayward pretty. Some men were. Her ex for instance. Perfectly groomed, well dressed, all of it screaming privilege. Never Brodey. Brodey was a man's man, rugged and strong and comfortable in torn jeans because that was who he was and accepted it.

Touch him. Go ahead. Why not? If it ended the way it had last night, she didn't imagine he'd complain. Giving her the invitation she needed, he closed his eyes and she moved closer, trailing her fingers over that perfect nose. He flinched and nearly got his eye poked for his troubles.

"What?" He rubbed his nose. "A fuzz or something?"

"No. I wanted to touch you. Really, I want to sketch you, but I don't think you'll let that happen."

"Good guess there." He waggled his eyebrows. "I'll let you do other things to me."

Such a man. "I'm sure you would. As soon as we finish going through these reports and you tell me I can rip up that laundry room. Ticktock, handsome. With each day, I see my bonus—and my assistant—slipping away."

"You're saying if I let you rip up that floor, you'll have sex with me?"

She laughed. "This is what it has come to. I'm bargaining myself for a laundry room."

"You can rip up the floor."

What? She pulled back an inch, opened her mouth, closed it again. *Really?* "Are you teasing me?"

"No. I'm not. Whatever was in there is gone now. I have to accept that and let it go. Tear it up. Let's see what's under there."

LEXI'S HEAD DIPPED forward and Brodey bit the inside of his cheek to keep from laughing. "I know it's shocking, but try to control yourself."

Her face—that gorgeous face that kept him awake at night—lit up, all perky and relieved, as if he'd just handed her the assistant she'd otherwise kill for.

"Thank you, Brodey."

He leaned over, dropped a light kiss on her lips. "The crime-scene people went through it again today when they grabbed the quilt. There's nothing there that'll help us. But we've got the break-in at your place, the quilt and the link between Ed Long and the Williams family. Now we figure out if that link goes further than the defense attorney and how. There's a reason Long is checking you out. He's nervous."

And people who were nervous had something to be nervous about. Particularly criminals. But according to his rap sheet, Ed Long wasn't a violent guy. Unarmed robberies made up his sheet.

Hold up here. Brodey lurched forward, ran his hands over the financial statements on the coffee table, shuffling through them. *Pfft, pfft, pfft.* Nothing. He moved to the next stack.

"What are you looking for?"

"There are no SAR reports."

"SAR?"

"Suspicious activity report. *S-A-R*. They're reports on funky transactions. Filed by financial institutions—banks, brokers, you know—and sent to the Financial Crimes Enforcement Network. FinCEN. It's part of the Treasury Department and helps the Feds identify terrorists and money launderers. Law enforcement can get subpoenas for copies of reports from FinCEN. Helps us figure out if a suspect is moving money around."

"So if the banks think something is hinky, they fill out one of these SAR reports?"

"Yes."

"Can anything trigger the report?"

He shrugged. "Anything suspicious, yes. The banks watch for patterns. If someone suddenly deposits six grand every week after only depositing hundreds for a while, that could trigger it."

Lexi picked up one of the bank statements. "The dollar amounts are all over the place. There's no pattern."

"That could mean this is a dead end or it could mean Williams knew—because he was a broker and would have been familiar with SARs—if he kept to his pattern it wouldn't look suspicious."

Lexi threw her shoulders back, smacked him on the arm. "Yes! The SAR would have jeopardized his Ponzi scheme if investigators checked his finances."

He touched her nose, grinning at her because—holy hell—he might be crazy about this woman. "I love intelligent women."

Obviously wanting to play, she tapped his nose. "*I* love intelligent men. Especially ones who offer to sleep on my sofa—instead of trying to get lucky—so I don't have to be alone."

"But I did get lucky."

"After you said you'd sleep on the sofa. See how this works?"

Brodey cracked up.

Again she reached over, ran the tips of her fingers along his jaw, and that feeling, that surge of power, ripped through him. If she sensed it she didn't care because that hand kept roaming over his face.

"Please let me sketch you."

Maybe he could work this sketching thing to his favor. "What do I get out of it?"

She hopped up and grabbed her sketch pad. "You'll get something. We can talk while I'm sketching. It helps me think."

"Right. Sure. Just don't spread it around. This gets out, I'll never live it down."

Lexi sat across from him, tucking her legs underneath her into her go-to sitting position. She glanced up at him, a tiny smile playing across her lips and—damn—he wanted to kiss her. He wanted to do way more than kiss her, which, if she lived up to her end of this sketching bargain, he'd be doing before the night ended.

While she kept busy, he leaned back, focused on the financials and possible next steps. All these random numbers could have been Williams trying to fly under the radar. But what about Brenda? She had to question their money being moved. He glanced at Lexi, whose hand flew across her sketch pad. "I wonder how involved Brenda was in maintaining their household accounts."

"Meaning, did she know about all these transactions? Lift your chin a bit. Not too much… perfect."

"According to Jenna's notes, Brenda didn't know about the Ponzi scheme. But if she even looked at their bank statements she'd have seen the constant movement."

Lexi shrugged. "If I married a broker, I don't know if I'd question it. And Jonathan Williams was slick. I mean he swindled people out of millions of dollars and they didn't know it. Convincing his wife of something would be simple. She loved him and trusted him. It's easy to be fooled by someone you love."

That, he knew, was her voice of experience, but this time, when she mentioned her ex, she didn't sound as…what? *Affected.* That was it. Score one for Team Brodey if she was ready to move on from her former idiot fiancé.

"And the bank wouldn't flag small transactions—small to Williams anyway."

Still sketching, she waggled her free hand. "Turn a little to the left."

Seriously? What was he? Some kind of art experiment? He rolled his eyes.

"Brodey, don't be a wuss."

He turned left. "Just warning you, I'm cashing in when this is over."

"As if that'll be horrible?"

He grinned, loving this casual banter between them. He could thank scumbag Ed Long for that at least. Had he not allegedly—God forbid a detective should accuse someone of something without adding *allegedly*—broken into Lexi's place, they probably wouldn't be sitting here cracking jokes about getting lucky.

"Ed Long," he said.

"What?"

"I missed something."

He sat up and riffled through the reports on the coffee table until he found one from the month before the murder.

"Hey! I wasn't done."

"Sorry, babe."

She set the sketch pad down. "What is it?"

"This guy isn't the brightest bulb. He's also, as we know from him skipping on his rent, strapped for cash."

"And?"

He held up the report. "And we need copies of his bank statements to see if any of the transactions on Williams's bank statements match Long's. My guess is if the bank suddenly sees Long depositing large amounts they're going to—"

Lexi smacked her sketch pad on her leg. "File a SAR."

"Yep."

"How do we get that information?"

"We tell McCall to get a subpoena."

Chapter Twelve

"Hayward," Brodey groaned into his phone.

He blinked a couple of times, working the morning fog from his brain while he focused on the fact that McCall was calling him at six in the morning. A morning that came after another night of shortened sleep thanks to the beautiful, if not sometimes annoying, Lexi Vanderbilt.

"Junior," McCall snarked, "you gettin' soft since you been on leave? Get the hell out of bed."

Beside him, Lexi rolled over, her arm flinging sideways and blasting him square on the beak. Yikes. It was like sleeping with a circus act. Slowly, trying not to wake her, he shifted sideways, got to his feet and went to the still-dark living room, where the Chicago dawn had yet to do its magic and light the place up. "What's happening?"

"Got your subpoena for the SARs. Sending

it over now. Also got one for his bank records. Bank opens at seven. I'm heading over there."

"Okay. You going back to your office afterward? I'll swing by."

"Yeah. I'm out."

The line went dead. Apparently that was the end of the conversation. Brodey tossed his phone onto the couch in the general vicinity where he'd left his clothes the night before. He'd never again be able to look at that couch without picturing Lexi sprawled across it. Naked.

Waiting.

Yes, sir. Helluva night.

She wandered into the room wearing only a tank top and a pair of skimpy underwear. Definitely no bra. *Good morning, sunshine.* She bumped the wall and dropped a few other choice words. "Stupid wall."

Brodey snorted. "I see you're cranky in the mornings. You kiss your mother with that mouth?"

"All the time. It takes me an hour to wake up. If I could mainline coffee I'd do it."

Good to know for future mornings. What a switch this was, concerning himself with her morning habits. Something to get used to for sure. He blew air through his lips. "I have good news for you."

She threw herself across the couch, landing

on top of his clothes and phone, and curled into a fetal position. "What is it?"

"McCall got the subpoenas. We'll have financial reports on Ed Long this morning. What's your schedule? Besides letting me take you back to bed?"

That got a smile out of her. "Why?"

He smacked her on the rear and ran the backs of his fingers down her thigh, then back up again as he formed a to-do list for the day. "Because I'm meeting with McCall to go through these reports. I can get my dad to hang with you, but I know he's got an appointment at nine. I'd like to park you somewhere safe until he can get there."

"Brodey," she said, "you're not parking me anywhere. I have two potential clients today. Both on the North Side. Big opportunities. And I'm not missing them. Bad enough I can't keep up with my voice mail. I'm not about to start blowing off new opportunities."

"Lexi," he said in that same don't-be-an-idiot tone she'd hit *him* with, "I'm not asking you to blow off clients. I'm figuring out how to keep you out of trouble while you meet with them."

She stretched her legs and rolled to her back and—*oh, mama*—could he figure out a way to marry this woman without having to wake up to her cranky moods each morning? Maybe he could leave for work before she got up. And since when did he want to marry anyone? Much less a crabby, sexy-as-hell interior designer.

She sat up, stretched her arms over her head and—yeah—that tank top didn't leave a lot to the imagination. "Sweetheart, as soon as we finish this conversation, I'm taking you back to bed and putting a smile on that crabby face."

"I thought you were in a hurry."

"I am. Sometimes being in a hurry is more fun. Now, what's your schedule?"

She stood, walked over to him and hooked her arm into his, leading him back to the bedroom. "My first appointment is at nine. It's a high-rise with a doorman. You can drop me off. The other one isn't until noon."

"My dad will take you. I'll call him."

"Can we not talk about your dad right now?"

"Honey, we don't need to talk at all."

McCALL SLAPPED A manila folder, its edges perfect and untorn, on top of the scarred veneer table in the PD conference room. At least they'd moved from the interview room this time. In the battle of stale odors, the antiseptic smell in this room beat the hell out of sweat any day.

"Anyone asks," McCall said, "you were here for a visit. You get caught near this evidence, we'll be pulling answers from our rears. I'm not risking evidence getting thrown out because a defense lawyer got wind you saw it."

Brodey set his hand on the file and dragged it across the table. If McCall was anything like him, when he received new evidence, he stored it in a new folder. The folder McCall just unloaded? That sucker was too perfect—too new—to be old evidence. "Understood. Whatcha got?"

"Junior, your hunch paid off. These are your SARs on Ed Long."

Yeah, baby.

McCall tossed another folder—this one tattered and ripped. "I also found another set of financials. They were in the bottom of the box. Someone shoved them into a separate folder. Drives me crazy."

"More financials?"

"Yeah. A second money-market account. Brenda was a cosigner but he was the only one who signed the checks. We pulled copies of every one. No Brenda."

"Maybe that's the account he was moving all the Ponzi scheme money through."

"Could be. *Millions* moving through that account."

Inside the newer-looking folder Brodey found four separate SAR reports on Ed Long, each containing his address, Social Security and driver's license numbers. Farther down was the good stuff. The details of how and why a SAR had been triggered on one Edward G. Long. Brodey skipped over the second section to the bottom of the page and the three rows of check boxes. Beside each box were options on different forms of suspicious activity—bribery, identity theft, check fraud. The only box checked on this particular report indicated a significant transaction had occurred for no apparent purpose. Meaning, Ed Long deposited money— four times—in a manner completely out of his normal pattern.

And, lookie here, the date range of the suspicious activity occurred three weeks before Jonathan Williams, financial fraudster, met his maker.

"Now we're talking."

"What?"

From his messenger bag, Brodey grabbed the copies of the financial reports he and Lexi had reviewed the night before and spread them on the table. "These are Williams's bank statements. Tons of transactions, big and small. This guy was obsessed with moving money. I'm thinking if we can match any of his transactions to Ed Long's SARs, it's worth taking another look at the loving wife."

McCall scooped up the financials and dug a

pen from the inside pocket of his sport coat. "I follow. Give me the dates on the SARs and the transaction amounts."

"First one is for nine grand. November 5."

McCall scanned the pages and let out a low whistle. "Nothing."

"Damn. Nothing even close?"

"Well, there's a few in that range, but they're odd numbers. Eight thousand one hundred and twenty, nine thousand five hundred and fifty-five. Nothing in flat amounts. You didn't think we'd get that lucky, did you?"

Yeah, actually, he had. But this was detective work and why he loved it.

Performing the same exercise, they reviewed all four SAR reports. No matches. *Son of a gun.* He knew—knew—there had to be a connection here. Call it instinct, call it a hunch, call it whatever, but in that moment Brodey understood how detectives got tunnel vision. How they sometimes followed a path that didn't necessarily add up, but still managed to make a case. All along, from the day he graduated from the academy, he'd sworn he wouldn't be one of those cops who didn't keep an open mind.

Until now.

He sat back, breathed in. *Get it together here.* The other folder, the beat-up one, sat untouched. Another account that apparently Brenda Williams had never signed checks on. Something itched the back of his neck and he slapped his hand over it. "We're sure Brenda Williams never did anything with that money market?"

McCall gestured to the folder. "Check it yourself."

Sure would. He sat forward, shoved the SARs aside and opened the other folder. "Give me that pen." McCall tossed him the pen and Brodey went to work, scanning the money-market account's statement. When he hit the dates for the end of November, just a few weeks prior to the murder, he slowed his scanning, read each date, then checked the dates on Ed Long's SARs. No exact matches. But they were close.

Check the amounts.

Quickly he scanned the amounts, sliding the tip of the pen down over the column of numbers.

Nine grand.

Holy hell. Two days before Long deposited nine thousand dollars into his bank account, someone withdrew the exact amount from Jonathan Williams's account. Boom. The itch at the back of Brodey's neck turned to a full-on burn that lit his entire body.

"I got something." He circled the amount and the date on the money-market statement and slid it across to McCall. "It's a match. Could Williams's wife have forged his signature?"

McCall's lower lip shot out. "I guess. Check the other SARs."

Brodey grabbed the reports, laid them out in front of him and matched the three additional amounts on the SARs—all totaling fifty thousand dollars—to funds taken from the Williamses' account. He slid them across the table to McCall, who studied them for a few seconds.

The seasoned detective banged his knuckles on the table. "Son of a—"

"We got her. Somehow she withdrew fifty K from their money market without her husband knowing it. She had him murdered."

McCall pushed back from the table. "Time to *chat* with the grieving widow."

"Yep."

McCall pulled a face and slouched back, shaking his head. "Junior, you gotta sit this one out. I'm sorry. You can't be anywhere near this."

As a general rule, competition ran hot between detectives. Who caught what case, who closed how many cases, who got what convictions, it never ended. Brodey wanted to believe he was innocent in the whole thing, but—nah—he could be a dope among dopes when it came to one-upping another guy.

In this instance, hard-nosed McCall, King of the Dopes, appeared genuine in his apology for drop-kicking Brodey. "I know," Brodey said. "Call me when you're done."

LEXI FINISHED HER morning appointment with the Baldwins just before ten-thirty and marveled at her luck. Not only that, but also the appointment went well—seemed to anyway. One could never tell. The extra good news in this trifecta of luck was she had time before Mr. Hayward— her *bodyguard*—arrived to shuttle her to her noon appointment.

She stepped off the elevator at the lobby level in the Baldwins' high-rise and her heels tapped against the marble floor, echoing in the three-story entry. The doorman rushed to open the door, but Lexi pointed to the corner where three leather chairs—dark chocolate, simple, but elegant design—sat unoccupied. "My ride won't be here for a while. Do you mind if I wait in here?"

Because if she waited outside, aside from a solid case of frostbite, one Brodey Hayward would have a mental breakdown over the risks involved with standing on a street in Chicago. In daylight.

The doorman nodded. "Of course, ma'am."

"Thank you."

She set her briefcase and sample book on the floor next to her chosen chair, the one pointed away from streaming sunlight. A good dose of sunshine during a Chicago winter was nice, but not when she didn't have sunglasses to cut the glare. Sitting down may have been a mistake. Particularly since she'd slept only a few hours the night before—thank you very much, studly Brodey—and fatigue suddenly pressed in on her. With the extra time, she could close her eyes for a few minutes. Enjoy the quiet.

Phone calls, Lexi.

Endless phone calls that hopefully one day soon her assistant would be fielding. Between the potential bonus from the Williams project and possibly landing one of the two clients from this morning, she'd be able to afford the assistant and a small renovation on the garage.

And more than five hours of sleep a night.

Well, if Brodey let her sleep. She hummed to herself and the image of what they'd done on her now-not-so-virginal sofa heated her cheeks. God, the man's passions ran deep. He did everything—yes, everything—with intensity.

Phone calls, Lexi. Banishing thoughts of Brodey, she let out a long, satisfied sigh. Phone calls meant happy clients, happy clients meant more revenue, more revenue meant an assistant, an assistant meant free time to spend with Brodey and all his magical intensity.

Phone calls it is.

On cue, her cell rang. *Happy clients.* She dug

in her coat pocket and checked the screen. Ah. "Hi, Brenda."

"You witch!" she spat, the word stabbing like a ten-inch knife.

Lexi lurched back, her shoulders slamming against the back of the chair. She checked the phone's screen again in case she'd seen the wrong name. Nope. Brenda Williams. "Brenda? Are you all right?"

"Do I sound all right? I was just visited by a detective. Someone named McCall. Apparently, that other detective you hired has stirred things up."

Uh, she hadn't *hired* him. Maybe her connection to Mrs. Hennings got the ball rolling, but Lexi wasn't the one who agreed to let them help with the investigation. Although, this didn't seem to be the time to argue that. "What happened?"

"He walked in here and asked me if I murdered my husband!"

Lexi gasped, but Brenda kept rolling.

"It's not bad enough that I'm dealing with the fallout from his crimes—the humiliation and betrayal alone—never mind trying to explain it to our children. And now this? You brought that Jenna and her brother into my life and now I have the police accusing me of murder."

Energy spewing, Lexi shot out of her chair

and paced in small circles, around and around, rubbing her head with her free hand. "Brenda, wait, please. This is obviously a mistake."

"You bet it's a mistake. And it's one that better get resolved before they arrest me. And what about my children? I trusted you and now I need a lawyer!"

"Okay. Hold on. Please. Let me talk to Brodey."

Brenda made a huffing noise. "Absolutely not. You've done enough. All I need from you are the keys to my house."

"I'm sorry?"

"You're fired. I want the keys to my house here by noon today. Or I call the police and tell them you refused to give them back. Then it's on to social media, letting this city know what you've done to me. Noon, Lexi. Don't think I won't do it."

A sharp *click* sounded. "Brenda?"

No response.

No, no, no.

Lexi stared at the phone in her hand, her blood racing and yet fierce cold turning her feet numb. *Call back.* As upset as Brenda was, even if she answered, there'd be no reasoning with her. The clock on the phone blinked: 10:58 a.m. One hour until her next appointment. One hour. In that time, she could cab it home, grab the keys and run them to Brenda's house. While there she'd talk to her. Get Brenda to calm down and understand that even if she had connected her to the investigators, she didn't control them.

One hour to do all that and get to her next appointment. "Who am I kidding?" she muttered.

Damn it. All she'd done was try to help. To give a grieving widow some answers. And this was what she got? She got *fired*.

Because of Brodey.

No. He wouldn't do that. He wouldn't blindside and *humiliate* her this way. If he knew about McCall, he'd have warned her.

Buried somewhere in this mess she'd find a logical explanation.

Please let there be an explanation.

"Ma'am," the doorman said, "are you unwell?"

Unwell. One way to put it.

This was not happening. She'd worked too hard to allow this fiasco to destroy her reputation.

There goes the assistant.

"I'm fine," she said, grabbing her things. "Thank you. Would you be able to get me a cab, please?"

While waiting on her cab, she called Brodey. The truth was always somewhere in the middle and she needed his version. Then she'd talk to Brenda again. No problem. Misunderstandings happened all the time.

That was all this was—a misunderstanding.
She hoped.

By the third ring, he hadn't picked up and her
stomach did a vicious twist. She tipped forward,
drawing deep, even breaths—*don't freak out*—
until the pain leveled off.

Please answer your phone.

A slight *click* sounded—he'd picked up—and
the pressure in her belly released. *Thank you,
thank you, thank you.*

"It's Brodey. You know the drill."

Voice mail.

Refusing to panic, she focused on there being
a logical explanation for him not picking up her
call. He was a good man. He wouldn't ignore
her. Any number of things could be occupy-
ing him.

The beep sounded and she straightened, determined to battle the hysterical female control-
ling her body. "It's me," she said, hating the
pathetic tremble in her voice. "I need you to
call me back. Brenda Williams just fired me."

Ten minutes later and a block and a half from
her house, the cab came to a halt in the middle
of snarled traffic. *Can't get a break today.*

She grabbed a twenty from her wallet and
shoved it over the seat. "I'll jump out here. I
can walk the rest of the way. Keep the change."

On her tight schedule, she wasn't about to

wrangle over change. She hauled her sample book and briefcase out of the car and did a quasi-run-walk down the block. Sample books were not made for carrying long distances, and halfway to her cottage, she stopped and swapped everything to the other side. A blast of frigid wind smacked her cheeks and she sucked tiny ice picks of air.

Her phone rang. Scooting sideways, she dumped her sample book on the ground and scrambled for her cell in her coat pocket. Brodey. Excellent. Now they'd straighten this thing out and she'd prove to herself she didn't have rotten taste in men.

"Hi," she said. "Where are you?"

"Where am I?" he snapped. "Where are you? My dad was early and the doorman at the address you gave him said you left."

Just one second here. She'd gotten fired and he dared take an attitude with her? Really?

"I'm on my way to my house to retrieve the key to the Williams place. Brenda demanded I return it by noon. After she *fired* me."

"You should have waited for my dad. You can't go there alone."

Oh, please. As if she had time for one of his annoying lectures. And had he even heard she'd been fired? He'd completely blown by that fact when he should be thanking her for not going ninja on him. For restraining herself when all she wanted was to demand answers and beg him to tell her he hadn't humiliated her.

"Well, Brodey, I don't have the luxury of waiting for an escort. I have clients to see. Considering I just lost one because your friend Detective McCall went to her house and accused her of killing her husband."

"Stop it. He didn't accuse her of killing him."

So he knew.

Fueled by her damned heart splitting in two, a burst of anger soared and she gritted her teeth, fought the rage shredding, absolutely dismantling her from inside out. God, how did she have such colossally bad judgment with men? Honesty shouldn't be a lot to ask for.

She stared at the cars moving through the intersection, focused on the movement, the various shades of blue and silver and red, and brought her mind to a place of detached calm. "You knew about this and didn't tell me?"

"Lex, it happened fast. When was I supposed to tell you?"

"Uh, maybe when you decided she was a suspect?"

"Come on. You knew I hadn't completely ruled her out. You *know* the wife always gets a look."

Now he wanted to weasel out of it on a technicality. And worse, manipulate her into thinking this was her fault because he hadn't shared information with her. He could have at least warned her this might happen. She'd trusted him to do the right thing, to not keep things from her, to not *betray* her. Instead, she'd been blindsided. She may not have walked in on Brodey with another woman, but he hid things from her, and a lie by omission was just as devastating.

Once again, she'd allowed a man to humiliate her.

And break her heart.

Foolish, foolish woman.

"Don't even, Brodey. You never told me things were moving forward on her. Or that McCall was going there today. Frankly, I can't blame her for firing me. I'd probably do it, too. You knew what I had riding on this project, and now she's blaming me because you and your detective buddies accused her of murder. You could have warned me!"

"Why is she blaming you?"

Ugh. Idiot man. "Because I brought you into this! She thinks if you weren't involved, the case would be stalled."

Still holding the phone, she slid her briefcase to her shoulder and scooped up her sample book. The left side of her body would be a war zone after hauling all that weight, but right now, that was the least of her issues.

"She'll calm down," he said. "I'll have Jenna talk to her."

"Oh, you'll have Jenna talk to her? Why, thank you. That makes me feel *so* much better."

A car flew by the intersection and beeped at a truck stopped at the corner. That would be the capper of the day; getting mashed between two vehicles. She'd just hook a right and cross at the other end. Away from this traffic.

"What's that honking?" Brodey asked.

"Cars. It's a city. We have them."

"Are you gonna knock it off with the sarcasm and let me explain?"

"What's to explain? You knew she was a suspect and didn't tell me."

"It's an investigation."

"Oh, oh, oh, it's an *investigation*. Funny. You weren't saying that last night when you had me stripped naked on my damned sofa! You lied to me. I trusted you to do the right thing. God help me, I always pick the liars."

"What?" he roared, his voice so loud she yanked the phone from her ear. "Do not lump me in with that scumbag."

Lexi sucked in a breath at the outburst. Brodey had a temper. Even if she'd never seen it in action, she'd sensed its swarming presence, waiting to be unleashed.

Well, she'd apparently set it free.

"Don't yell at me."

"And what? You want me to sit here and let you compare me to that cheating piece of garbage you almost married? *That's* what you think of me?"

No.

Yes.

So confused. Continuing her trek down the street, she shook her head, blinked back tears. "I don't know what I think."

"Then you need to figure it out. I didn't lie to you, Lexi. I'm not even supposed to be investigating this thing. I'm on leave. My involvement could seriously screw up this case. If they bring charges against her, I'm gonna have to answer for it. I could lose my damned job."

"Now that's my fault, too? I didn't tell you to get involved. Talk to your sister about that. In fact, I don't want to hear from you anymore."

"I'm a homicide detective. There are things related to cases I won't be able to share with you. It comes with the territory. You want full disclosure all the time, and as much as I'd like to do that, I can't. Simple fact."

And, wow, didn't that just sum up their biggest issue. Yes, she wanted honesty. More than that, she deserved it. Clearly, he didn't understand that. "I trusted you and you…you…you *disappointed* me. Brodey Hayward, you broke my heart. And that, I won't tolerate."

Chapter Thirteen

"Lexi!"

Brodey dragged the phone from his ear. Call Ended. Damn it. She'd hung up on him. And eee-doggies the woman was steamed. Well, hell, so was he. After all this damned work, she'd compared him to a lying, cheating scumbag. As much as he enjoyed her, *craved her*, that was a no-go and he really would be a liar if he didn't admit the whole scenario got him riled.

Temples throbbing, he stood on the sidewalk in front of the coffee shop where McCall had given him the what's-what on his talk with Brenda. A fight with Lexi, he didn't need today. Suddenly, his professional and personal lives were crumbling into a hot mess.

Take a breath. Yeah, a minute to regroup. Focus. Get organized.

He inhaled, drew in the filthy fumes from a city bus—just his luck—and released the poison from his body. *Regroup.*

From what McCall had told him, there were no accusations made, but Brenda Williams wasn't stupid. The minute the detective started asking about the suspicious transactions, she'd shut him down, which meant she had something to hide or she'd panicked.

Maybe both.

With the timing of Lexi's call, Brenda must have called her the minute McCall had left. Who else had Brenda called? *Think like a criminal.* Had it been him who'd hired Ed Long to kill his spouse, old Ed would be next on the call list. She'd want to alert him, close ranks and make sure they had their stories straight.

And Long had already tried terrorizing Lexi. Seemed both Brenda and Ed wanted to blame her for their screwups. A siren blared, bringing Brodey out of his mind and he turned to see a patrol car whipping around a cab and screaming through the intersection. Sometimes he missed patrolling and that shot of adrenaline that happened when the sirens wailed. Sometimes. Most times, he'd take a good, complex investigation.

Right now, he wanted to do a time reversal, go back to the day when his sister asked for his help and tell her to beat it, that he wasn't risking his career for something that would wind up being a pain in the chops.

Yeah. As if he'd ever do that with Jenna. He

loved his baby sister too much for that. And she knew it.

Women.

He took two steps and froze. *Lexi's on her way home.* If Brenda had called Ed Long…

A stream of pavement-melting swearwords flew from his mouth. An older woman standing on the corner gasped and shot him a horrified look.

"Sorry, ma'am!" he hollered as he ran by.

His feet hammered against the sidewalk and the joint-shattering pounding shot straight up his legs to his bum elbow. Nothing but issues today.

He'd parked three blocks over. From there it'd take him fifteen minutes, if he got lucky, which wasn't typical lately, to get to Lexi's. She could call him paranoid all she wanted, but if Long had tried scaring her off before they'd had any solid evidence, what in the hell would he do if Brenda had broken the news about a paper trail?

At the second corner, a man pushed the button on the light pole and waited for the walk sign. Forget that. Brodey angled around him and jumped off the curb, where a cabbie screeched his brakes in an attempt to not tattoo Brodey to the pavement. Brodey held up his hand and kept running. "Sorry, dude!"

He stopped at the adjacent corner, his breaths coming in short, hard bursts from the sprint.

Ignore it. He inched his way into the street, his elbow howling as traffic whizzed by. He'd be in that sling for a month after this. *Come on, come on.* Finally traffic cleared and he darted across the intersection. With only a block to go, he alternately scanned the sidewalk in front of him—no one blocking his way—and scrolled for his dad's number. There. He hit the button.

Voice mail. Of course. "Dad, get over to Lexi's. She's on her way there. So am I. I'll explain later, but bring your sidearm."

LEXI DUMPED HER briefcase and sample bag at her front door and dug out her key. Between the lack of sleep and the emotional onslaught of the past thirty minutes, a sob gurgled in her throat. Blasted man. After a night of pure sin, ecstasy to the highest level, he'd duped her. But, no, she would *not* cry. Damn him. He'd had her thinking maybe, just maybe, he could be trusted. That he wouldn't hurt her. Not intentionally anyway. And he'd done it. All he'd needed to do was be honest with her. Instead he'd lied. He knew what the Williams project meant to her, that she'd finally be able to afford an assistant and have some kind of life again, sleep a few extra hours a night and not die of a stress-induced heart attack anytime soon. And he'd disregarded that. Tossed it aside like last week's moldy bread.

And that might be worse than finding her fiancé with his intern.

She slapped her hand against the front door, and stinging pain rocketed into her palm up her forearm. *Brilliant, Lexi. Way to make it worse. The heck with it. I'm crying.* Why not? After the week she'd had, she deserved a good healthy cry. She flipped the lock and shoved the door open. Immediately, the annoying *beep, beep, beep* of the alarm filled the house, scraping against her eardrums like sharp nails. Thirty seconds. That was how much time she had to punch in the code. *Beep, beep, beep.* She grabbed her sample bag and briefcase, dragged them over the threshold, kicked the door shut—*beep, beep, beep*—and reached for the keypad. *Beep, beep, beep.* "I know, I know. Just shut up."

Before this week, life had been so simple. Busy but simple. No annoying beeps from the alarm, no ugly keypad marring her perfect walls, no man making love to her on her precious sofa.

No strangers invading her house.

The door. She hadn't locked it.

"Shoot."

Beep, beep, beep. She tapped in the code, silencing the alarm—*thank you.* Something squeaked. Oh no. An instant prickle skidded straight down her spine. She hadn't locked the damned door.

She turned toward the door, her body moving slower than her brain would like until finally... *Oh God*.

Ed Long stood in the entryway, his cold, dead eyes squinting at her. Fear stormed her, spreading everywhere at once, her heels, her legs, her arms. Then, as if taunting her, it slowed, prickling along, making her shiver until it reached her neck.

She stepped back, her body moving of its own accord, wedging her between the outside wall and the man blocking the front entry.

Back door.

The front door would be useless. She'd have to get through him to escape. Plus, she had heels on and he'd easily catch her. But she wouldn't stand here having a conversation. Whatever he wanted wasn't good. Not if he'd murdered Jonathan Williams.

Slowly, she slid out of her shoes and he smiled at her, his crooked top teeth flashing. She'd missed that the first time. Not this time. But that menacing look let her know that he knew she'd run.

Which she did.

She tore sideways, her socks slipping on the floor, but she'd gotten a decent jump and focused on the back door at the end of the short hallway.

Almost made it, too. Just past the kitchen, he grabbed hold of her coat, yanking hard and tugging her backward. Momentum knocked her off balance and she swayed left—*don't fall, don't fall, don't fall*—before toppling over.

Still he hung on. She scrambled, her feet sliding against the tile as she tried to get up.

"No, you don't," he said.

"Please. I haven't done anything. Just leave. I won't call the police."

"Too late for that, isn't it?"

He jerked her to her feet, pain blasting her shoulders. On the way up, her arms rubbed against his jean-clad legs, and the stench of his soap, something cheap and medicinal, burned her throat.

"I warned you." He shoved her, hard, and she flew against the sofa, the edge of the arm connecting with her ribs. Ow. Knifing pain sliced into her and the tears started again.

"Please," she screamed, praying someone outside, maybe Mrs. Jenkins, who heard every tiny thing, would hear her.

But he grabbed her again, scooping her up around the waist and tossing her onto the sofa as if she weighed nothing. For a skinny man, he was strong. *Too strong to fight.* Getting away would be her only chance.

"Get out!" she hollered again, still praying for the miracle of her nosy neighbor.

He smirked. "She's not home. I saw her go out half an hour ago. Lucky me, I got a parking spot two doors down. Been waiting on you, Lexi. And now we'll have some fun. And then your boyfriend is next. You two are causing way too much trouble."

Rolling sideways, she got to a sitting position and he leaped on her, straddling her in the exact spot where she and Brodey had made love last night. The image burned in her mind and she smacked at Long, flailing against him when he tried to grab her hands. She landed a punch, right in the chest, startling him for a few seconds. *Groin.* Fist still at the ready, she snapped her arm out.

And connected.

Yes. Her attacker reared back, teetering on the edge of her knees and howling enough that her ears should have bled. He covered his crotch and—*push*—she shoved. One good thrust that sent him tumbling backward, his arms pinwheeling as he tried to catch his balance the second before he landed—*fwap*—flat on his back on the floor.

One chance she had to run and to get out.

She bolted off the couch, made it as far as the hallway that led to the back door before he caught her again. To her right stood her beloved Wedgwood vase. The one she'd been so concerned about after the first break-in. The one that made her realize the intrusion wasn't about money. Ed Long gripped the waist of her slacks and she smacked at him. No good. Too strong. He yanked her to her knees and she hit the floor hard, every bit of that hit blasting through her legs. *God, help me.* She kicked out and her heel connected with his jaw, startling him enough to give her a few seconds. She reached up, grabbed the neck of the vase with her right hand and swung. Whoosh! It bounced off his shoulder. She kicked out again, followed it up with another swing of the vase and, *boom*, clocked him. Right on the head. The vase shattered and its delicate pieces flew, sprinkling over the floor and creating a path of broken glass she'd have to run on. Lexi clawed at the wood and a sharp shard pricked her skin. She winced but leaped to her feet.

And ran.

Back door. So close. Right there. Locked. Got it. Before she had even stopped running, she had her hand out, ready to flip the new dead bolt Brodey had installed. Short, heavy gasps filled her lungs and her head spun from the oxygen burst. She reached for the lock, flipped it and swung the door open.

Frigid air hit her cheeks, brought her mind to a hyperfocus. Just ahead, the side of her garage and the back alley came into view. Get there.

Oooff. A huge weight landed on her and something dug into her shoulders. She went down, crashing to the path leading to the garage, and pain exploded in her hip. "No!"

God, she couldn't get away. So close.

"I'm done messing with you. That boyfriend of yours is talking to the cops. He sent one of them to Brenda's."

And his voice, low and gravelly and angry, fired another burst of panic. Lexi smacked her hand against the pavement. "Help me!"

Now on his feet, he gripped her arm, powered her to her feet, and she finally got a look at him. Blood streamed from the side of his head where she'd clocked him with the vase and a red mark stretched over his jaw where she'd kicked. She'd done some damage. *Do it again.* She would not die on one of the coldest days of the year. Why that should matter, she had no idea, but no. She would not have it.

As tired as she was, she'd hit him again and again and again.

"Let's go." He yanked her toward the garage. "In here."

Not the garage. If he took her in there, she'd never come out. That she knew. And there were enough tools—hammers, axes, saws—from the previous owner to do some real damage.

Just a foot in front of them was the side door to the garage. He kicked out, his heavy boots decimating the hollow door. "Inside. Now."

Another shove sent her stumbling and she sprawled across the cement floor, her hands taking the brunt of it. A few scrapes wouldn't be the worst of it if she couldn't get out.

Once again, she pushed off the frozen floor and got to her feet. Pricks of icy cold shot into her sock-clad feet and up her calves. She screamed again, raging at her attacker, wanting to claw his eyes out. Beat him worse than she'd already done.

Suddenly the assistant she'd wanted so badly didn't matter. Her growing business didn't matter. Brodey lying to her didn't matter. None of it mattered.

Not if she died.

"Why are you doing this? I didn't do anything."

"Yeah, you did. This case was dead. Cold as they come. For two years. And then you got nosy and put that damned flyer up. You stupid, stupid witch, you should have stayed out of it."

"Whatever Brenda told you—"

"Brenda didn't tell me anything. I don't even *know* her."

His gaze skittered around the garage to the assortment of tools hanging on the walls, sitting on metal shelves or in piles on the floor. Only a small open space remained where all the junk hadn't cluttered together. Closest to him was the workbench and he picked up a rusty screwdriver, ran his hand over the head.

"The plan was flawless," he said. "Flawless. He dies, she collects the money and everyone's out of hot water. No jail for him, no debt for her." He stroked the edge of the screwdriver, then switched hands, stroking it again and again. "Twisted as it was, the plan worked. Until you came along." He shook the screwdriver at her. "And I'm not going back to prison because of you."

SOMEONE SCREAMED.

Two houses down, Brodey heard it. *Outside.* Lexi. Rear of the house. Panic flooded his already bursting veins. Get there. He picked up the pace and again the pressure shot right to his bad elbow. He cut around the edge of the house, bumping the gutter hard enough that it crunched. The sound reverberated in the alley. Way to draw attention to himself.

He hauled down the narrow alley between

Lexi's cottage and the neighboring house, easing his steps as he reached the end. He stopped, peeked around the side of the house and scanned the patch of yard. The single-car garage to the left faced the back alley where cars and garbage trucks had access. From his spot, he couldn't see a side door, but the path from the house dead-ended and most of these old garages had an alternate entry.

No Lexi.

Where was she? Inside? Down the alley? Where? He whipped back against the house and squeezed his eyes closed.

"Shut up!" a man shouted from inside the garage.

Gotcha. Brodey visualized the garage. Single car. One large cargo door. Possible side door with a paved path leading to it. Lexi had told him the space was stuffed with junk from the old owners.

"Please," Lexi pleaded.

A door slamming cracked the air and then all sound ceased, leaving an eerie quiet that punctured Brodey's skin. He glanced around. No one at the back door, which only confirmed there was a side door to the garage.

Time for reinforcements. He dialed 911, identified himself, gave the dispatcher Lexi's address and hung up. No time to talk.

He poked his head around the side again. More muffled voices. One deeper—Ed Long; one higher and in a quick, panicked staccato—Lexi. Only two voices. If luck was on his side and it was just the two of them in there, he and Lexi would outnumber Long. A definite plus considering his injured wing and lack of side-arm.

Time to go. He slipped around the side, staying low as he hustled the short distance to the garage. Pressing close to the wall, he moved to the edge of the dwelling and peeked around. Entry door. Lock? No way to tell. Either way, he had to bust in there, go with the element of surprise and hopefully take Long down before he knew what the hell had hit him.

Still plastered against the house, Brodey inched around the edge, reached for the door-knob, wincing when it caught and clicked.

The door smacked open and he came face-to-face with—yep—Ed Long. Holding a screwdriver. Eyes darting, Long lurched backward, his face littered with that wide-eyed panic Brodey had seen on criminals a thousand times. With panic came irrational decisions. Time to go lights-out. Instincts roaring, Brodey swung, knowing it was going to hurt. The uppercut connected with Long's jaw and made a gut-twisting crunch. Long reeled backward, farther into the garage, arms flying. The screwdriver sailed through the air and he grabbed the edge of the workbench to break his fall. Lexi stood in the middle of the only clear space but hopped sideways and—damn it—went the wrong way. Now wedged into the far corner, her mistake must have hit her because she looked at Brodey, her perfect face drawn and pale and haunted.

"Run, Lex!"

Brodey went back to Long, still righting himself near the workbench, where strewn across the top was every form of weapon—pickax, screwdriver, hammer, a *vice*—Brodey could conjure. Great. A burst of sunlight filtered through the garage door windows, illuminating the interior. He scanned the junk-filled space. Shovels, rakes, extension cords were stored in every available spot. He shifted right, closer to the shovel. One good swing and any weapon Long chose would be knocked loose.

"Brodey?" Lexi said, still standing there.

"Run!"

Long lunged for her, his weapon of choice an ice pick he'd found in the rubble, and Brodey snapped. At that moment, he envisioned Lexi, that pick butchering her, and he knew, no doubt, he'd kill this man to save her.

Brodey dodged left, blocking Long's path to her as he swung the pick, his arm thrusting upward to run it through. Brodey raised his good arm, blocked the swing and kicked. *Boom.* His boot skittered across Long's knee. Brodey pounced, shoving him backward, away from Lexi. The pick came at him again, but the block was late and, oh, hell, the tip nicked him, drawing blood.

Long laughed. And it wasn't one of those sinister ones Brodey had seen in movies as a kid. This laugh was casual. Entertained. Somewhere along the way, Ed Long had gone seriously off his rails.

"Brodey! Back!"

Whoosh. Something flew in front of him and hit Long dead center in the forehead. A spade. Lexi had hurled a garden spade at him. Good for her. It bounced off his head, but drew blood before clattering against the cold cement floor. Long stared down at it with a dazed look that could have been surprise or unconsciousness calling him. He reached up, touched his head where blood trickled, then brought his eyes to Brodey's. Crazy eyes. *Desperate* eyes. And desperate eyes might be the most dangerous of all.

Any heat in Brodey's body disappeared, replaced by frigid chills. He stepped forward and Long came at him again. Brodey circled right, trying to pin his opponent to a corner as they squared off. His foot hit something. Big. He shot a look at it. Fire extinguisher. Compliments of Lexi, something else flew at Long. This time Long was ready and leaned right as a hand shovel arced by him.

He lunged for her.

Extinguisher. Brodey grabbed it with his good hand. If he could get the pin out...but his other arm hung limp at his side from that first crack at his opponent. He bit the end of the pin, yanked it out and hit the handle.

"Lex, move!"

Half a foot from Lexi, Long spun back and a spray of foam hit him square in the chest. Brodey aimed higher. Bingo. Long let out a howl that should have cracked the windows, a long, piercing sound that shredded the musty garage air.

Finally, Lexi darted past him, heading for the doorway.

But she stopped. "Seriously?" he hollered.

"What can I do?"

What could she do? If they lived through this, he'd kill her. "Get the hell out!"

Long rubbed at his eyes, trying to clear the stinging foam. *Go ahead, buddy, rub it all in there.* Brodey grabbed him by the shirt, hauled him the two feet to the workbench. And Lexi, once again ignoring his directive, moved beside him.

"I told you to get out."

"Shut up. Let me help."

Stubborn woman. Fine. "Stand over here. By the vice."

Long swung at her and Brodey, still hanging on with his good hand, kneed him in the thigh. Hard. Long howled. Quickly, Brodey let go, clamped on to his hand and shoved it into the vice attached to the table. "Close that," he yelled. "Fast."

She spun the lever and Brodey watched the sides squeeze against Long's hand. The man howled again. Not tight enough. He could see Long sliding his hand around, playing them, planning his counterattack.

"Shut up," Brodey said. "Keep going, Lex. Two more turns."

After the second spin, he checked the tension on the vice. Good enough. It would at least hold Long until they could tie him up. First, he'd have to get rid of the handle so their prisoner didn't get any ideas about reaching over and loosening the tension with his free hand. Brodey unscrewed the handle and held it in front of Long's face. "You're cooked."

"We'll see."

Ignoring the taunt, Brodey shoved the handle into his back pocket. Long kicked out. Apparently, that caused a whole lot of problems for his hand because he howled again. "Please, man. Let me outta here."

So much for his cocky posturing three seconds ago. "Forget it. But tell me what you did and I'll loosen it. Give you a few seconds to catch your breath."

Sirens filled the sudden silence and Brodey cocked his head to judge the distance. In this city, they could be going somewhere else. Who knew? But how about that, the sirens grew louder. Time to up the stakes on Long. "Dude, I couldn't care less if you talk. But the cops are gonna be here any second, and the way it looks to me is you and Brenda Williams murdered her husband. You're both going down."

"No!"

"Yeah!" Brodey mimicked his squealing voice.

Long swung his head back and forth so fast it should have flown off. Or at least paralyzed him. "She didn't have anything to do with it," he said.

"Right. Really heroic, but there's a money trail. The detectives didn't figure out the trail led to you until you came after Lexi. Now it's done."

"It wasn't…"

Brodey turned to the door, jerking his thumb at Lexi to get out. "Save it for your lawyer."

"She wasn't involved. She's a good mother."

Blah, blah, blah. He'd heard it a hundred times. "Yeah, I know. What was it? An affair? You and Brenda?"

"No."

"Police!"

Long's panic escalated. His gaze shot to the doorway, where Lexi stood, taking it all in, and then he came back to Brodey, again shaking his head hard enough to scramble what little brains he had.

"I swear. It wasn't her. It was him. Jonathan. He gave me a key and told me to kill him."

Chapter Fourteen

Lexi stood by the door, hands curled into fists at her sides, letting her attacker's words sink in. Not in this lifetime would she consider herself a good detective, but this was beyond reason. This insane man who'd terrorized her expected them to believe Jonathan Williams planned his own murder.

"Chicago Police!" a man yelled from outside the door.

Lexi spun sideways, holding up her hands "It's okay," she said.

"I'm Detective Brodey Hayward," Brodey called from behind her. "I'm with Area Central."

"Step outside," the cop closest to Lexi told Brodey. "Show me your hands."

Brodey did as he was told. Weapon drawn, one of the cops stepped into the garage, while the other covered them. If she never again saw the barrel of a gun pointing at her, she wouldn't mind. Right now, after the storm of emotional horror she'd just experienced, her body was too deflated, too spent to feel much of anything.

She slid her gaze to Brodey, whose eyes were on her with that same intensity she'd learned was so much a part of him.

"You're fine," he said. He addressed the officer. "This man is Ed Long. He just attacked Ms. Vanderbilt. I arrived in the middle of it. Detective McCall from Area North is working the Jonathan Williams murder. Long claims he killed him. We need to get McCall here. Fast."

WHILE THE POLICE did their thing in her garage, Lexi went inside, searching for the comfort of her favorite chair. Sketch pad in hand, she worked with colored pencils, drawing random items for who knew what. Brodey sat across from her on the sofa, their sofa, and she dared not look at him. If she looked at him, he'd try to talk to her, and she couldn't do it. Couldn't form the right words to tell him what she needed to. That she'd been terrified and he'd saved her from Ed Long's torment and she would forever love him for it. But her emotions right now couldn't be trusted. Her *emotions* told her to walk over to that sofa, to Brodey, and curl into him. Cry it out. Take comfort from him and in him because he'd opened up a part of her that had been dead for almost a year.

And it would be easy to do. To just let go.

Only it wouldn't fix the fact that she needed—no—demanded honesty in a relationship and he, given what he did for a living, would never be able to truly open up to her. Some things would stay buried inside him and that, she knew, would terrorize her worse than Ed Long ever could.

So she remained rooted in her favorite chair doing her favorite thing, trying to pretend this was any other day. Sketching was about therapy. About keeping her mind and hands active while she worked through the stress of the situation unfolding before her. Even if her trembling fingers wouldn't allow for anything decent to be created, at least she'd be distracted from thoughts of what happened, and could have happened, in her garage.

The back door creaked and she looked up to see Detective McCall enter the house.

"Well," he said, "this one I haven't seen."

"Tell me," Brodey said.

McCall dropped onto the arm of the sofa, folded his arms over his chest. "This guy is unhinged. According to Long, he met Jonathan Williams through his lawyer. He was doing odd jobs at the lawyer's house and Williams came to pick up his kids at a playdate. Isn't that what it's called these days?"

Lexi nodded.

"Anyways, Williams hired him to do some work at his place. Nothing inside. Yard work, stuff like that. When the Feds closed in on Williams, he panicked. Guy like him? He can't do time. Doesn't have the spine for it. And if he went away, his wife, they were on the outs, would be left in one hell of a jackpot. Between the debt and what the scam victims got robbed of, even if they got divorced the wife would be busted."

"So, he wanted to what? Kill himself?"

McCall rolled out his bottom lip. "Not exactly. He wanted to take care of his kids. Give the mope credit for that. Suicide doesn't get an insurance payout, though. Turns out, our boy Long here is a family man. Believes a man should protect his family above all else." McCall snorted. "Gotta love that."

"And with no insurance money," Brodey said, "the wife and kids are stuck with the debt he'd racked up. She wouldn't even get the house. The government would seize everything."

"Unless he was murdered," Lexi added.

"Unless he was murdered." McCall circled his hand at Brodey. "Those withdrawals we thought Brenda made? Williams did it. He took the money out and paid his would-be assassin. Then Long deposited the money, and with amounts that high it triggered the SARs."

"And here we are," Brodey said.

Lexi was finally maxed out from trembling, and her pencil slipped from her hand and fell to the floor. "The man had himself murdered."

Brodey whistled. "Makes sense. Williams gives Long a key, tells him to sneak up on him in the house and kill him."

"Close," McCall said. "According to Long, he was supposed to show up the next day, but he's a career thief. Murder isn't his specialty. Williams paid him and he started to get cold feet. One night he gets banged up on a bottle of Jack whiskey and goes to the house a day early. Uses the key to go in the side door. Williams hears a noise and comes to check on it. Long startles him and—" McCall formed a gun with his fingers "—bang. Job done."

The man had actually done it. Absolutely horrifying. Lexi uncurled her legs and sat forward. "That explains the broken glass. He must have been carrying it when he went to the laundry room." She turned to Brodey. "Just like you said."

"What about the address book Lexi found?"

McCall shrugged. "Don't know. My guess is Jonathan hid it in the wall, but when Dr. Doom showed up early, he didn't have a chance to get rid of it. It's a helluva mess."

"We stirred things up again."

"Sure did. For the last two years, Long's been keeping an eye on Brenda and the kids. Heck of a guy, this one. He saw you coming and going and followed you to the house last week. If not for you, maybe he'd have gotten away with it."

Somehow, that didn't make Lexi feel better. Maybe they should have left it alone. Brenda Williams would have been debt-free if they had. But a murderer, albeit a murderer who wanted the kids to be cared for, would have gone free.

Later, after a month of sleep, Lexi would weigh the moral arguments. Hopefully, she'd decide they'd done the right thing by solving this case. Right now, Brenda and her kids and the emotional fallout they would again endure made her wonder.

Brodey turned to Lexi, waited for her to meet his gaze. Yes, she was mad at him and didn't think that would be even a remote possibility.

IN THE HOUR since McCall had left, Lexi moved to one of the counter stools, attempting to choke down a glass of water. Well, what was left of it after she'd sloshed it all over herself. No matter how hard she pressed her fingers against the glass, literally willing herself to relax, every little inch of her still trembled. She glanced up at her precious sofa that she'd taken such extreme care not to damage, where she'd finally allowed herself to be a little careless and made love to Brodey. Her precious sofa where she'd been pinned down, fighting for her life.

Forget it. She set the glass on the counter and pushed it away. Water wouldn't control this chaos.

The front door opened and Brodey stepped in, quickly shutting the door behind him and blocking the blast of cold overtaking the room. He took three steps, then stopped. In the short time they'd known each other, he'd learned her *stay back* signals.

"You okay?"

Was she? Hard to tell. Someone had tried to kill her. What were acceptable emotions after that? Fear, anger, panic? All of the above? At a loss for an answer, she remained silent.

"I know you're mad at me," he said.

Mad at him. Yes, she was that. She was also thankful and confused and...heartbroken. She'd fallen in love with a man who kept things from her. Unfortunately, she'd had enough of men like that in her life.

The door swung open again—her home might as well be Union Station at rush hour—and Jenna marched in wearing a long coat, boots and a knit cap and scarf. She looked as if she'd just hopped off a fashion magazine cover. Brodey, ever the gentleman—most of the time—shut the door for her.

"Hey, guys," she said. "Dad called me."

"Hi," Lexi said, suddenly feeling as if someone had opened a pressure valve and let some of the tension out. Being alone with Brodey brought more confusion and she was too hyped up, too *conflicted*, for that.

Jenna, at this moment, was Switzerland.

She may have been Brodey's sister, but she was a woman and understood a woman's emotions. Lexi patted the stool next to her. "Come sit."

Crossing the room, she took her coat off and set it on the arm of the sofa. That damned sofa. Lexi glanced back at Brodey, who had most certainly recognized his sister had been invited to sit, but not him. His eyes were on her, their gazes holding for a long moment, and the sadness rolling between them sawed right through, just tore into Lexi's flesh with agonizing speed. She blinked a couple of times, trapping tears she refused to let loose. Not now. Maybe later.

"I'll let you two talk," Brodey said, his gaze still locked with hers. "I'll call you later. Please answer your phone."

Oh, how he'd gotten to know her. It would be so much easier to walk away again. All this hurt and anger needed time to simmer. Eventually, maybe, they'd be friends. Now, she couldn't trust him. The ultimate death blow for any relationship.

She watched him turn away and open the door. "Jenna," he said, "lock this door."

Always so diligent. That was Brodey.

Jenna hopped off the stool and secured the door. Then she spun on Lexi and narrowed her eyes. "What was that about? I thought you two were, I don't know, dating or something."

Or something.

"We were."

"Past tense?"

"He lied to me."

Her eyebrows hit her hairline and she crossed her arms. "My brother is a nudge, but he's not a liar."

Little sister had gone into battle mode. Lexi reached back for her abandoned water and drained it. "Thank you."

"For what?"

"Before you walked in here I was shaking so hard I could barely hold this glass."

Jenna made her way back across the room, slid onto her stool and patted Lexi's leg. "I know what happened in the garage. My dad told me while you were talking with the cops. Now you're mad at Brodey. What happened? And don't tell me he lied. I don't believe that."

Being an only child, sibling loyalty was foreign to Lexi, and having never experienced it, she hadn't missed it. But the idea of it, that unconditional acceptance, she suddenly wouldn't mind having. "Let's say he lied by omission. He knew McCall talked to Brenda about her possible involvement in her husband's murder. He knew that and he didn't tell me. I was blindsided when Brenda fired me."

"She *fired* you?"

"Yes. If I hadn't talked to Mrs. Hennings about you helping on the case, none of this would have happened." She ran her palm up over her forehead. "Good God, what is wrong with these people that they blamed *me* for all of this? I didn't hire Ed Long to kill Jonathan Williams. How is it all my fault?"

"It's not. That's dumb. Ed Long is a criminal and Brenda is a single mother whose nerves took over. When she gets the full story, she'll hire you back."

Lexi shrugged. "I'm not even sure it matters."

There goes the assistant...

"Of course it matters. It's not right. As for Brodey—"

"Please don't defend him."

Jenna sighed, then scrubbed her hands over her thighs. "I won't. Well, maybe a little, but not in the way you think."

"Seriously?"

She held her hands out. "Just hear me out. I grew up surrounded by cops. I'm still surrounded by cops. Now it's worse because my boyfriend is a US marshal. You think Brodey won't talk about cases, try dating Brent. He's a vault."

"You poor thing," Lexi said.

"You have no idea. Anyway, my dad worked homicides as long as I can remember. Some nights he came home miserable and quiet. It took me years to understand he couldn't talk about his job. He kept his investigations to himself. Maybe he shared some things with my mom, I really don't know. But otherwise, he kept it all to himself. He always worried he'd somehow let something slip and it could blow his case. Brodey grew up with that, too."

"But he knew how important honesty was to me."

"So, it's not about you getting fired, but about him keeping it from you?"

"Yes! If he keeps something like that from me, what else will he keep from me? I walked in on my fiancé—a man I adored, a man I thought was honorable—getting busy with his intern."

Jenna's mouth opened wide enough to drive a truck through it. *"Really!"*

"Yes, really. Do you know how humiliating that is?"

"I'd have shot him."

"Wish I'd thought of that."

"Oh, honey. I'm so sorry."

"It's old news. Better I found out before I married the pig. But honesty is a hot button for me. Everything needs to be on the table. And your brother knew the Williams project was important to me and he let me be blindsided. Worse, he didn't trust me enough to believe I could keep quiet."

Jenna inched her head back and forth. "I don't think that's true."

"Well, what other option is there? And don't tell me it's his job. I understand that. This wasn't just any case. I had personal implications in this. I sat in Brenda's living room and vouched for him. And convinced her to trust him. I helped convince her to let her children look at a sketch of the man who murdered their father. He should have figured out a way to warn me. He didn't have my back, and I can't be with a man who doesn't protect me emotionally. As protective as your brother is, he is clueless when it comes to emotions. He doesn't get it, and for me that's a major thing not to get."

"You should talk to him."

"What good would it do? How do we get

beyond him choosing what I should hear or not hear? If it involves me, I'm entitled to know. I'd do it for him. That's what I know."

They sat quietly for a few minutes. Lexi waited for an argument, but none came. At least one of the Hayward siblings understood her. Either that or Jenna simply didn't want to argue.

Lexi could budge on a lot of things. This was not one of them.

BRODEY PUSHED HIS dad's recliner back and settled in to watch the Bulls. Might as well. The fresh injury to his elbow had earned him another trip to the doctor and four more weeks of physical therapy, so he didn't have anywhere else to be tonight. Four more weeks of loafing around, doing nothing but thinking about Lexi's silent treatment.

In the next hour, his mom would remind him he was a single man sitting idle on a Saturday night and he should get a life. Then she'd throw his butt out. But for now, he'd delay venturing into another arctic night. Being here with his family meant avoiding going home to his empty apartment—and empty bed—to obsess about Lexi.

Three days had passed since they'd spoken. Outside of that first night when he'd called to check on her and she'd told him she was fine—

he hated that word—she'd gone to radio silence. Their one conversation had been brief. Was she okay? Yes. Did she need anything? No, thank you. Was she still mad at him? Yes.

"Damn," he muttered to himself.

They had the Williams case all wrapped up and Ed Long would spend a good chunk of his life in prison. Who knew what would happen with the Feds? They'd probably seize the home and auction it to make reparations to the fraud victims. Brenda Williams wouldn't get a dime. The insurance company might even go after her for the money it'd paid out on the life-insurance policy, but at least everyone had answers. Even if the answers stunk.

"Hey," Jenna said from the doorway leading to the kitchen. "Mom just set out pie. If you're interested, you'd better get in there before Brent and Dad destroy it."

"Nah. I'm good. Thanks. If there's any left, I'll take a piece home." He turned the volume up on the game.

"Nice try."

"What?"

"You want me to leave you alone." Jenna held her thumb and index finger up to her forehead. "*Loser*. Why would you even think that trick would work?"

Brodey sighed. "I'm tired. Go eat pie."

She sat in the other recliner and turned sideways to face him. *Yeah, she's not going away.*

"What's happening with Ed Long?"

"Lawyered up. He'll probably take a plea. He's still going away for a long time."

"Did you let Lexi know?"

"Tried."

"She's still mad at you, huh?"

"Don't know."

"Have you talked to her?"

He gave her a hard look. "See, that's the thing. Talking to someone requires that they return your calls, which she won't do. Short of stalking her at her house—not a banner idea—I'm out of options. You need to call her and make sure she's using the alarm. Every time she leaves, she needs to set it."

"And you wonder why she won't talk to you?"

What? His face suddenly got hot. He'd had a hell of a few days with women either telling him all the things he'd done wrong or, worse, not saying anything at all. "What does *that* mean?"

"All you do is nag about how she has to be careful. Not everyone thinks with a cop's mind. And apologize for keeping that Brenda Williams thing from her."

Here we go. Bad enough he had to explain himself to Lexi, who, as a matter of fact, wouldn't *let* him explain. Now he had to report to his sister. "It was an *investigation*. I was supposed to tell her and risk it getting back to Brenda? Come on. You know better."

"Yes, I do. I also know that maybe you could have figured out a way to warn her. Brodey, you're such a dope."

"Hey!"

"She's not mad because she got fired. She's mad because you didn't trust her. Right or wrong, she thinks you lied to her or that you kept things from her. With her history, it's a hot button. You need to apologize. Not because you didn't tell her. That's a tough call. Apologize because you didn't trust her enough to tell her there were certain things you couldn't share. That's what she needs to understand. To her, it looks like you betrayed her to solve this case."

He snorted. Women. "Wrong."

"Is it? What's she supposed to think? The first time you met Brenda, you tagged along with Lexi. Then you asked her to help sketch the crime scene and even review the financial reports. She convinced Brenda to trust you. She had faith in you, and when things broke loose you chose not to tell her what was happening. I know what I'd think."

"That's not what happened. And the Brenda thing wasn't my fault."

She slapped her hand on her thigh and stood.

"Justify it however you like, but unless you figure out a way to get Lexi to understand, you're gonna be sitting in Dad's chair by yourself for a long time."

"Listen, Jenna, don't hold back."

Damn, he was tired of people accusing him of messing up. She bent over, kissed him on top of his head, shocking the hell out of him because she'd never done that before and he wasn't sure what to do with it. Although, after the rotten few days, not to mention his mother constantly bugging him to get a life, he didn't mind Jenna's sudden burst of compassion.

"You're a ding-a-ling, Brodey, but you mean well. Eventually, she'll see that. If you really care about her, and I think you do, don't give up."

Dishes clattered in the kitchen and Brodey glanced behind Jenna, where Brent and his dad waited for their pie to be rationed.

"Babe!" Brent hollered. "You want pie?"

She glanced over her shoulder, a small smile lifting her lips, and Brodey's heart slammed. His sister was in love. Knocked out, slam-dunked in love. And Brent was a good guy. Perfect for her in every way because he managed to not put up with her nonsense *and* take care of her at the same time. As happy as that made him, something pinged inside him. With Lexi, he'd had a taste of it. Not enough. Not the full-blown experience as his sister had. Suddenly, he wanted it. Hungered for it.

"Do you have any idea," Jenna said, "how much I love it when he calls me *babe*? I never cared for it before. Hated it, in fact. It always seemed so...I don't know...sexist. Now? I can't go a day without hearing it. From him. Only from him."

"He loves you."

"Yeah, he does. And he makes me happy." She set her hand on Brodey's shoulder and squeezed. "I want this for you. I want you to know what it feels like to have someone love you that much. Don't give up."

DAY FIVE WITHOUT Brodey proved to be just as miserable as days one, two, three and four. At least he hadn't called today. Was that a good thing? Lexi didn't know. It hurt to see his name on her phone, to hear his voice when he left messages, and now it hurt worse to *not* hear his voice.

At the ugly core, thinking about Brodey simply hurt.

So, she'd gone back to doing what she did best. She worked. From dawn until evening, she reviewed samples, created sketches, caught up with clients and had even managed to land the client she'd seen on the day of Ed Long's arrest. Which meant, without a doubt, she could afford to hire an assistant.

She punched in the alarm code, silenced the annoying beep and set her briefcase in its usual spot next to the locked door. Thanks to automatic timers, the house was well lit. Never again would she walk into a dark house.

A murderer had taught her that.

Her phone whistled. A text. Before taking off her coat, she glanced at the screen. Brodey. So much for him not contacting her today. A text, though. Usually he called and left a voice mail. *Don't read it. Let it go.*

Would it hurt less if she ignored it? Probably not.

She tapped his name on the screen and the message popped up.

Can you come out back?

Out back? An eruption of excitement banged against her chest. Was he here? Putting her thumbs to work, she replied.

You're here?

Yes.

Oh, boy. How did she feel about this? She took a second and closed her eyes, then breathed in and out a few times before responding.

I don't want to fight.

If she knew nothing else, *that* she knew.

We won't. I want you to see something.

What was this man up to? She dropped the phone on the coffee table, went to the back door and peeped out. The darkening sky winked with a few scattered stars, but she could see him in front of the garage, hands shoved into his leather jacket, no hat. As cold as it was, he had to be freezing. She threw the door open. "What are you doing? It's freezing out here."

"I've only been out here a few minutes." He jerked his thumb. "I was in there."

"The garage?"

"Yeah." He waved her over. "I want to show you something."

"Brodey, what are you doing?"

"Just look. I promise I'll go after that."

Still in the doorway, she glanced back inside, down the long hallway, where that blasted sofa she could no longer sit on, much less look at, taunted her. Whatever this was out in the garage, she needed to face it. And finally tell Brodey she couldn't stand hearing his voice every day. That he had to give her time. Time for what, she didn't know, but all the crying over the past few days destroyed her energy.

She clutched the top of her coat closed and stepped outside, where frigid air burned her lungs. "Brodey, it's so cold. You shouldn't be out here."

He led her down the path to the side entrance to the garage. Four days ago, this garage had been hell.

"Close your eyes," he said.

"What are you up to?"

"Close 'em. I'll guide you in. Don't worry."

After shutting her eyes, she held out one hand and he grabbed it, gave it a squeeze, and the connection, the boost, zipped up her arm. A ball of heartbreak jammed in her throat and she swallowed once, then again—no good—as he led her forward.

"One more step," he said.

But she knew that because the arctic air had been replaced by warmer air inside the garage. "Did you put a heater in here?"

"Yes. You can look now."

She opened her eyes, let them adjust to the interior light and, without moving her head, did a quick scan. Spotless. All the rusty tools were gone; the others, probably the salvageable ones, hung on hooks on the walls. The workbench sat in the far corner and shelves had been mounted above it. Nice shelves, too. Not the cheap ones. She stood there, taking it all in. Even the floor had been cleaned. Sure, there were still stains, but the dirt, every bit, had been scrubbed away.

"Oh my…"

Brodey held his hand out. "What do you think? Are you mad?"

Was she *mad*? For two years she'd been wishing she had the time to clean out the garage. And after the torment they'd faced in there, she'd all but decided that damned garage would continue to be her own personal purgatory. "You did this all today?"

"Yeah. Well, I had help. Jenna and Brent took a day off and my mom and dad helped. With the bum wing, there's no way I could have gotten it done in one day. I wanted to start yesterday, but I didn't know if you'd be home. Today, I knew you'd be gone all day."

"Where's all the stuff?"

"Uh, in the trash. Most of it wasn't usable. We saved everything else and moved it to the storage place down the block. Figured you'd want to go through that yourself. At least now you can use the garage for something positive. Put the… uh…other stuff behind you. Did we overstep?"

She reached for him, squeezed his arm. "Of course you did. But I love it. It's amazing. Thank you. You didn't have to do this."

"Yeah, I did."

"Brodey—"

He faced her, grabbed her hand before she could pull away. "Wait. Please. Just one second. Let me talk and then if you want me to go, I'll go. Okay?"

She nodded.

"Great. Perfect. Just have a little patience. I pretty much stink at this."

"You don't stink at it."

"Yeah, I do. Anyway, here goes. I know I hurt you. I'm sorry for that. It was shortsighted. I should have thought it through and explained why I couldn't tell you about Brenda. Should have had that conversation early so you'd know certain things are off-limits. I could give you every reason I've come up with about why I couldn't tell you—and it's a long list." She smiled and it pushed him forward. "But it doesn't matter. All that matters is that I hurt you when I didn't mean to. I realize that now. I get it."

"Do you?"

"Yeah. I do. I didn't before. Shame on me. Now I know you need the communication.

Whether it's what you want to hear or not, you need it."

Five days ago, she'd have dropped to her knees and thanked heaven above for this gift. She might still. Was she a fool for wanting to believe him? The old Lexi would say yes. This Lexi? The one who saw Brodey's face every time she looked at the sofa wasn't sure. "I need to know I can trust you with everything."

"You can. Look, I've never…I don't know… I guess I've never had someone who cared about my job. I've had relationships, sure, but none that, well, mattered. I came and went and that was it. This situation is new to me. And I screwed up." He waved his hand around the garage. "This is my way of showing you I'm sorry. Whether you give me a second shot or not, I wanted to show you I can take care of you in every way. I get it. It's about physical and emotional security. My keeping the Brenda Williams thing from you was about my job. I didn't put you first. If I could go back, I'd handle it differently. I'd tell you things were happening with the case that I couldn't share, but that you needed to be prepared. I'd warn you just like you asked. I'm hoping you'll tell me that's good enough. What I do is hard, I'll always have secrets, but…"

"I know."

"You know?"

"Jenna told me about life with a cop. I see it from the other side now. Before, I couldn't. I wanted you to understand why I was mad, though. It wasn't about the case. Not really. It was more that the case was the catalyst."

He nodded. "I get it now."

She grabbed his jacket and squeezed. "Thank you."

"For the garage?"

"For everything. I've missed you. Every time I looked at the sofa, I wanted to put the thing out for trash. All I could picture was you sitting on it, and it hurt even more." She inched closer. "Promise me I can trust you. Please. I need that."

"You can. Absolutely. No doubt. We're good together."

"Even when you're lecturing me?"

He smiled. "Yeah. Even then. Heck, maybe you can teach me to lighten up. See what's good in the world instead of what's not so good." He backed up. "Oh, gotta show you something else."

What now?

He dragged her to the workbench and the unopened box on top of it. The box was about fifteen inches long and had a picture of a ship on it. The *Titanic*. God help them if he wanted to compare their relationship to the *Titanic*. She glanced up at him. "I can't wait to hear this one."

"I bought that. It's a model-ship kit."

"And?"

"You told me to get a hobby. To take up something that relaxed me. Like you have with sketching. I took your advice. I'm going to build model boats. I may even get this one done before I go back to work. So now you have your sketches and I'll have model boats. We can do it together when it's quiet. What do you think?"

She picked up the box, read the contents. "It's a lot of pieces."

"Yeah, but I like putting pieces together. If I could do it with you next to me, even better. What do you say, Lex? Want to build boats with me and show me what things can be instead of what they are?"

"Oh, boy, Detective. That sounds like fun."

He waggled his eyebrows. "I hope so because, honey, I'm just getting started."

* * * * *